# Also by Jan Springer

**Intimate Secrets**
Intimate Lover
Intimate Kisses
Intimate Stranger

**Kidnap Fantasies**
Jade's Fantasy
Zero To Sexy
Christmas Lovers

**Pleasure Bound**
A Hero's Welcome
A Hero Escapes
A Hero Betrayed
A Hero's Kiss
A Hero Wanted
Captive Heroes

**Pleasure Bound Boxed Set**
Pleasure Bound : COMPLETE SERIES SciFi Erotic Romance Boxed Set

**Tentacles Shifter Erotic Romance**
Taken by Him

**The Desperadoes**
The Pleasure Girl
In Her Bed
Awakening Eve

**The Key Club**
A Merry Menage Christmas
Sophie's Menage
Jewel's Menage
Jaxie's Menage

**The Outlaw Lovers**
Jude Outlaw
The Claiming
Colter's Revenge
Tyler's Woman
Resistance
The Outlaw Lovers
Alpha Outlaws Boxed Set

**Vampira**
Sweet Heat
Dark Heat
Wet Heat
Crimson Heat

## Standalone

A Touch of Menage Boxed Set
Shades of Menage Boxed Set
Naughty Girl Desires Boxed Set
Nice Girl Naughty
Sinderella Sexy
The Biker and The Bride
The Fire Within
Bared to Him
Pleasure Bound : A Futuristic Adult Romance Boxed Set
Merry Menage Kisses Boxed Set
Inner Girl Rising
Stripped Naked
Risqué Girl Delights Boxed Set
A Holiday Menage
Ménage À Trois
A Hitman for Hannah
Billionaire Boyfriend
Edible Delights
Vampira
Toygasm
The Dark Side

Watch for more at www.janspringer.com.

# Claiming Her Cowboys

Moose Ranch #6 ~ Cowboys Online #7

• • ✿ • •

*Jennifer Jane (JJ) Watson spent ten years in a maximum-security prison. The last thing she expected was to get an early release, along with a job on a remote Canadian cattle ranch caring for three of the sexiest cowboys she's ever met!*

• • ✿ • •

*Rafe, Brady and Dan thought they were getting a couple of male ex-cons to help out around their secluded ranch, but instead they get an attractive and very appealing female.*
*In the wilds of Northern Ontario, female companionship is rare so it's a good thing the three men like to share...*

• • ✿ • •

They're dominating, sexy-as-sin and they give JJ the hottest ménages plus one adorable baby!
But her second pregnancy comes as one giant surprise, and JJ's anxiety overwhelms her when she doesn't know who the father is.
Is it Rafe, Dan or Brady?
Spring days on this ranch are bursting with hard work, danger and emergencies but nights are filled with scorching passions and naughty pleasures as JJ lays claim to her three sexy cowboys.

S tories in the Cowboys Online Series:

Cowboys for Christmas ~ Book One – Moose Ranch #1 Cowboys Online #1 -Free

Cowboys in Her Pocket ~ Book Two – Moose Ranch #2 Cowboys Online #2

Loving Her Cowboys ~ Book Three – Moose Ranch #3 Cowboys Online #3

Cowboys In Her Heart ~ Book Four – Moose Ranch #4 Cowboys Online #4

Always Her Cowboys ~ Book Five – Moose Ranch #5 Cowboys Online #5

Her Forever Cowboys ~ Book Six – Snowy Creek Ranch #1 Cowboys Online #6

Claiming Her Cowboys ~ Book Seven – Moose Ranch #6 Cowboys Online #7

# Copyright

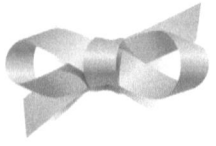

# License Notes

This book is licensed for your personal use only.

# Author Note

This is a work of fiction. Characters, places, settings and events presented in this book are purely of the author's imagination and bear no resemblance to any actual person, living or dead or to any actual events, places and/or settings.

# Chapter One

M *oose Ranch*
*June – Present Day*

"You're what?" Rafe questioned as his head snapped up like a jack-in-the-box from the oily tractor part he'd been working on at the barn workbench.

He gawked wide-eyed at JJ with apparent shock.

"What did you say?" Brady asked.

His eyes had narrowed with confusion as he tossed a bag of cattle supplements onto the barn floor. Then he placed his hands on his lean hips and stared at her with a stunned expression that instantly made her regret just announcing her news out of the blue.

"Can you say that again? I don't think I heard you right," Dan queried from his perch at the far end of the workbench where he'd been opening a package of organic fertilizer that he'd ordered for their outdoor garden.

JJ swallowed as nervousness embraced her.

She'd been sure they'd heard what she'd just said.

Well, maybe not.

She'd blurted her news the instant she'd entered the barn and realized all three of her cowboys were in here.

She knew she should have waited. Perhaps bake cookies and decorate with blue and pink icing to drop hints or tease them with insinuations of what she'd just discovered today during a secret trip to her doctor while flying into the city to pick up the supplies needed for the ranch.

But they needed to know, and truth be told she was a nervous wreck at what she'd just learned.

This was a total shock, despite her suspicions.

"I said, I'm pregnant."

Her confession had come out as just above a whisper, just as it had moments earlier. It was not the strong voice she'd planned.

The three men continued to stare at her as if totally not hearing what she'd just said. Heck, she must have looked the same way after her doctor had given her the news.

Brady was the first one who broke their stunned silence.

"Are you sure? I mean, we were all using protection. We weren't even trying to get pregnant."

He stopped abruptly and his eyes widened and his eyebrows raised in surprise as he continued.

"Unless...well...there was that time when the two of us were without protection...that was about...oh, shit," he said in a hoarse voice that made JJ's tummy drop as if she were on a runaway elevator.

Brady did not look happy.

"Actually, there was that one time earlier in the spring when we got carried away too and I didn't have protection..." Rafe slowly said and bit his bottom lip as he frowned.

Gosh, he didn't look pleased either.

"Oh man, and the condom broke that one time with the two of us," Dan mumbled and closed his eyes and exhaled a slow breath, as if trying to calm himself.

Another unhappy man.

*Oh, no.*

Anxiety rippled through JJ.

This wasn't the reaction she'd hoped for from the guys.

Sure, the pregnancy had been unplanned but she hadn't meant for any of them to feel trapped and right now they all looked imprisoned.

Their reaction certainly was not the same as when she'd broke the news to the men during her first pregnancy. Her first-born had been planned. She'd wanted a baby and she'd picked Brady to be the father, and he had agreed.

She wanted this baby too...she just hadn't wanted him or her quite yet and without knowing who the father might be.

"How far along?" Brady asked. His voice sounded gruff and strangled.

He didn't come close to her. Didn't appear over the moon with excitement like the last time.

None of them did.

"The doctor figures I'm about three months along," she admitted. She smoothed her hands over her belly nice and tight to show what she perceived was a tiny baby bump. Or maybe she was just wishful thinking?

Frowns deepened.

"How is that possible? You aren't even showing?" Rafe replied.

Wow. That was an insult.

"Are you sure it is three months?" Dan asked.

Irritation snapped through JJ.

It was very rare she got mad at one of them.

Sure, sometimes they stole her freshly baked cookies or cut into a cake before she'd had a chance to frost it. This, however, was not baked goods.

This was her baby. Their baby.

She just wasn't sure who the father might be.

Despite that fact, she wanted them to be happy. To be accepting.

To whoop and holler and lift her up in their arms and be happy.

"It is not an *it*. *It* is either a girl or a boy. A he or a she. I'll thank you to remember that. Supper will be ready in one hour. I'll expect you all to be cleaned up and ready to eat."

Despite feeling crest-fallen, she was proud she'd been able to muster her strictest voice.

Without waiting for any comments from the men, she turned and left the barn as fast as her feet could carry her.

When she was sure none of them were following her, she allowed herself to remain composed until she stepped into the mudroom of the ranch house.

And then she began to cry.

"Did she just drop a baby bombshell on us? Or was I hallucinating?" Rafe asked as he stared at the other two men who were gazing at each other and kind of looking like they were shell shocked.

"I think we pissed her off," Dan said.

"Not me, it was your comment about the baby being an *it*," Rafe protested.

No way was he taking the fall for making her mad. He'd never piss her off. At least not on purpose and if he ever did, it would be a teasing remark in jest.

"She said she's three months along. That means maybe another Christmas baby," Brady whispered.

"Maybe you're the dad again?" Rafe said hopefully. He did want a baby with JJ, he just had wanted it to be a private affair like it had been with Brady and JJ.

"Maybe *you're* the dad, Rafe. Protection, people. Protection." Brady shot back. His eyes were sparkling with anger and Rafe felt it crawl under his skin as well.

Brady had no right to be pissed off at him.

"If memory serves me correctly, you admitted to not using protection, so don't call the kettle black," Rafe shot back, his anger increasing.

"Easy, guys. We screwed up," Dan interjected in a calming voice that immediately settled Rafe.

"All of us did," Rafe admitted. "We got carried away. JJ is a beautiful, sensual woman. We all love her like crazy. There's no reason to panic. We have another baby on the way. It doesn't matter who the dad is. We all love Chrissy and we will all love the newbie."

"The newbie?" Both Dan and Brady said in unison, disapproving frowns on their faces.

"Hey, better than calling her or him an *it,*" Rafe replied, his anger raising again.

Geez, he needed to relax. There was another baby on the way. And it could be *his.*

*Oh man!*

"Shit, we're going to have to come up with names. Where the hell are the baby books? Anyone know?" Dan asked.

Brady and Rafe shook their heads.

"We're going to have to come up with a hell of an apology too," Brady said.

"Now that this surprising news has sunk in, I think I know why she didn't look happy when she left. And it was more than Dan saying the baby was an *it.* I think I know what we can do to make it up to JJ," Rafe said.

"What's your idea?" Brady asked.

It appeared he now had Dan and Brady's full attention.

"Come into my parlor, gentlemen, and I will show you my plan," Rafe chuckled as he headed into the adjoining barn office, suddenly feeling excited and happy.

"Yum, Yum, Yum. There you go," JJ cooed as she quickly pushed a baby spoon full of mashed peas into Chrissy's mouth. Her almost six-month old, blue-eyed, daughter grimaced, kicked her feet and clenched her pudgy hands in protest upon the highchair tray.

JJ held her breath as Chrissy moved the mound around in her mouth, throwing JJ an expression of "I'm not sure I like this stuff, but I'll give you a decision soon".

For a few seconds, it looked like she might spit out the peas, but thankfully she didn't.

"Good girl. I am so proud of you," JJ praised.

They'd slowly been introducing some solids to her baby. So far, she enjoyed mashed sweet potatoes and mashed steak. Just like her father.

JJ's anger and subsequent sadness toward the guys seeming unhappiness about the unexpected baby news had dissipated once she returned to the ranch house, had a good cry and then found her daughter lying down, awake and looking out of the playpen that had been set up in the living room for her.

For one brief instant, a dark, panicky thought had overwhelmed her. Her daughter had been left alone in an unlocked house. Someone could have come inside and kidnapped her. Or she could have choked on one of her toys strewn in the playpen or she could have somehow climbed out, fallen and injured herself.

But those scary scenarios had dissipated as reality set in. They were miles away from anyone. There was a baby monitor out in the barn so the guys could hear her. They had probably left her alone for a short time because she'd been asleep and they hadn't wanted to disturb her. All her toys were baby proof and she wasn't even able to stand yet.

But still...she should not have been left alone. Not for a moment.

Anxiety had worked its way into her with everything that had happened and she was trying really hard to distract herself in the hopes the uneasy emotion would fade away.

The food for dinner was almost ready and Chrissy still hadn't spit out her peas.

JJ blinked, not quite believing her luck. She had swallowed the peas and her lips were parted as if she wanted more!

This was too good to be true!

"Awesome! Here," JJ prodded as she dipped the utensil into the green mush. When she lifted the spoon, Chrissy had closed her mouth and looked at JJ with a mischievous glint in her baby blue eyes.

JJ feigned surprise.

"What? You don't want anymore? Oh, come on, if your baby brother or baby sister were out here, he or she would be chowing down all this delicious grub, I guarantee it, sweet pea."

To JJ's surprise, her daughter opened her mouth and JJ quickly pushed the green food in.

Chrissy closed her lips and happily kicked out her legs as she once again moved the food around in her mouth.

JJ laughed, happiness clutching her heart.

"Oh my goodness! I cannot believe it! We are going to have so many eating competitions!"

"And food fights!" Brady's amused voice came from immediately behind her.

JJ tensed and then twirled around to see him standing there. Her heart leapt at the smile on his face.

Hopefully he'd come around about the surprise baby news.

"I didn't hear you come in," she replied, trying to keep any kind of disappointment and sadness out of her voice.

But now she understood why Chrissy was suddenly eating. She always ate for her dad.

"You were so involved with the baby; the roof would have crashed in and you wouldn't have noticed. Man, am I ever thirsty," he chuckled as he headed into the kitchen.

He grabbed a glass from the cupboard and turned on the faucet.

Brady's offhand comment about the roof collapsing made an awful scenario of the ranch house roof caving in after a tree crashing through it. The thought sent shivers of dread racing up her spine and tingling into her scalp.

That anxiety she been trying to keep at bay, crept up a notch.

*It's just a joke, JJ. Don't take it so seriously.*

But she was taking it seriously. Even her breathing had become quicker.

"After a drink, I'll just wash up and be back to set the table," Brady said.

She watched him as his eyes closed and he drank the water. A feeling of excitement washed over her, pushing away her burst of anxiety.

Gosh, he looked so healthy. So tanned. So sexy.

She wished she could stay mad at him for not even mentioning her pregnancy just now, but he appeared cheerful, so maybe he was okay with the news.

As she watched him drink, his blue eyes suddenly popped open and their gazes clashed. He was smiling at her as his lips caressed the glass and he continued to drink and watch her with a sensual sparkle.

She swore his eyes were making love to her as he studied her.

When his glass was empty, he gently set it into the countertop, but continued to hold her gaze.

His look turned intense. Sexual.

Her pussy quivered with excitement.

"If you keep staring at me like that, you know what will happen," he said in a thick voice.

"No, I don't," she teased.

"I'll carry you up the stairs and have my way with you," he growled.

She swore Brady was about to take a step toward her when heavy footsteps clomped upon the steps of the ranch house. The mud room door creaked open and she heard Dan and Rafe's laughter.

Okay, they were happy too. This was a good sign.

"Hold that thought," JJ whispered to Brady.

Her voice sounded breathy. Too breathy.

Brady swore softly and he quickly left the kitchen heading down the hallway to the nearest bathroom to wash up.

JJ let out an aroused breath and returned to feeding her daughter.

"Wow that was close, wasn't it sweetie?" she whispered to Chrissy, who had closed her mouth once again, refusing to eat.

JJ sighed and shook her head as she thought about what had just almost happened between herself and Brady. Had the guys not been around, Chrissy would be in her playpen and Brady would be making love to her on the nearest bed, and she would be loving it.

Pregnancy hormones would be the death of her.

At this pace, she was going to be pregnant all the time!

Rafe couldn't help but cast quick glances at JJ as they ate. Now that she had made the baby announcement, he swore her breasts were a bit bigger. Maybe her cheeks were chubbier too. Even her eyes seemed brighter.

Was it too early in the pregnancy to notice these things? He didn't know. He'd have to stick his nose into one of those baby books and find out. This baby could be his and he suddenly wanted to know everything about this pregnancy.

Not that he hadn't been interested in the first one. He had been attentive, but he'd known the baby would be Brady's.

Not knowing this time around who the father could be seemed to make things more...intense.

He remembered after Chrissy had been born, there had been a few weeks of abstaining from sex while JJ's hormones had tried to get back in order. That hiatus hadn't bothered him. He understood why she needed a break.

But it had been a very rough time for him emotionally, because she'd been so sad and he'd felt so damned frustrated in not being able to help her.

Postpartum blues, the doctor and midwife had said.

Rafe had been concerned and uptight that she hadn't been her cheerful self. But then the sparkle had finally come back into her eyes and she had become herself.

Now, he was worried for her again. Would the same thing happen after this baby? Would she get sad again?

He wanted nothing but happiness for her. She had brought such joy into his life; he couldn't imagine having to live without her. If something bad ever happened to her...he would kill himself. He could not go on without her.

That thought jolted him.

"Earth to Rafe. Did you hear me?" Dan asked from beside him and he suddenly realized he'd been staring at JJ and she was watching him, a frown of concern on her face.

Shit. He needed to come up with an excuse. And fast.

"Oh, sorry. Zoned out thinking about those wolves out in the northeast pasture near Misty Lake. Was thinking one of us should stay up at the cabin there for a few days. Keep an eye on the cattle nearby. See if we can prevent more cattle from getting killed."

Brady and Dan were looking at him like he had just grown horns.

JJ grinned, obviously relieved. Her pretty smile made his heart do a really nice flip flop. Yeah, she was his core.

"That's what we were just discussing," Brady said with a laugh.

Rafe blinked as surprise washed over him.

"You were?"

Man, he had just picked that excuse out of the blue.

Suddenly Dan shoved away his empty plate and patted his belly.

"Damn good supper, as usual, JJ," Dan said.

JJ's cheeks blushed pink at Dan's compliment.

Gosh, she was so cute.

"I aim to please. Anyone want dessert?" she asked as she stood.

Suddenly from the living room, Chrissy started to cry out.

Poor kid. She wanted some attention. Most likely from her mamma, since she had been away several hours today, which reminded him, they needed to unload the supplies out of the plane tonight.

"Hold on sweetie. Just for a little while longer and mommy will take you outside," JJ cooed.

"You two go ahead. I'll get dessert," Rafe volunteered and quickly stood.

"I'll put on some more coffee," Brady said, taking Rafe's cue.

"And I will get started washing the dishes," Dan added.

It was the least they could do with everything JJ did for them. He pushed away from the table and began collecting the dishes.

JJ was glad the guys were cutting her loose, but she was not happy that not one of them had said a thing about her baby news. She quickly picked up her fidgety daughter from her playpen, hugged her pudgy warm body, kissed her on the forehead and strolled down the hallway.

Now that she had some free time, her entire focus was on Chrissy, who was squealing with excitement and kicking her legs against JJ's belly.

"You want some fresh air, don't you sweetie?" she asked Chrissy as JJ opened the mud room door.

A brisk, fresh pine-scented June evening wind blew against them and Chrissy giggled as she stared toward the lake.

"Want to go down to see the sunset?" JJ asked.

But she knew the answer. Chrissy loved the sundown on the lake. She had some internal clock and always seemed to know when it was near sunset time.

Sure enough, the sun was just about to touch the treetops in the western horizon. The puffy white clouds in the sky were tinged with delicate pinks, whites and baby blue colors, which made her thoughts once again return to her unborn baby and if he or she was a girl or boy.

The doctor had set up an ultrasound appointment, but that wasn't for a few weeks. And even then, did she want to know the sex or would she rather it be a surprise?

And who was the father? Brady? Dan? Rafe?

She worried her bottom lip as she hoped the baby would be healthy as she walked along the trail and then stepped onto the dock. Chrissy's eyes were wide with wonder as she stared at Moose Ranch's big, white floatplane anchored at the dock as they passed it.

"You like mommy's plane, don't you?" she asked softly.

Chrissy kept her gaze to the plane, but when JJ stopped at the end of the dock, her daughter's head spun around to look out across the lake. A smile whispered over her pretty plump lips and they both stared silently at the beauty.

Waves rippled over the water and the pink, white and blue colors glinted off the whitecaps.

A couple of loons bobbed about thirty feet away from them, but they remained silent as they watched JJ and Chrissy.

Then suddenly a beaver appeared not more than ten feet from the dock, only the tip of his nose peeking out of the water, leaving a V in its wake.

Chrissy saw it instantly. Her blue eyes widened and her mouth went into an O shape. Then suddenly a giant splash erupted as the frightened beaver slapped its tail upon the water trying to scare them away as it disappeared beneath the surface.

JJ chuckled as Chrissy giggled. Then she quickly returned her attention to the lake, her blue eyes bright with curiosity.

The sun slowly disappeared behind the trees, taking the brisk wind with it and in turn casting cool shadows over their surroundings. This was JJ's favorite part of the sunset. The brilliant display of colors, then the peaceful quiet as shadows reigned for just a little while.

With the sun gone, a cool chill swept over her and she hugged Chrissy tighter in an effort to keep both of them warm.

It was so hard to believe that she had spent so many years of her life locked away in prison. Hard to believe that her life had been consumed with anxiety and panic attacks while she'd been incarcerated. That she hadn't ventured out of her cell, except for mealtimes or sometimes exercise.

Coming here to Moose Ranch had slowly set her free from the demons that had held her captive. But she'd had to work so hard in changing her thought process in order to diminish her anxiety.

That she'd been able to manage her anxiety enough to fly a float plane, still surprised her.

She shook her head as she remembered when she'd begun to learn how to fly. She'd been in anxiety mode every time her teacher had flown in with the float plane. And now with this niggle of anxiety starting to once again grab ahold of her, she wasn't sure if life would ever get back to normal again.

Why couldn't she be at peace like those loons? Or like the beaver, before it had been frightened?

Why was she feeling so sad that the guys hadn't been joyous about the baby news? Why hadn't they said anything about her pregnancy at dinner?

Maybe she was being too hormonal? Or maybe she was just tired? Maybe she'd feel better tomorrow?

JJ blew out a tense breath.

Maybe.

Rafe stiffened with excitement as JJ suddenly turned on the dock. As she talked to Chrissy, she started to walk toward the ranch house.

Oops! He needed to warn the guys she was coming!

By the time he got back into the guest room / second office where the printer was spitting out sheets of paper, the guys were already gathering other sheets of paper that had been splayed out on the bed.

"ETA about two minutes," he warned them.

Brady and Dan cursed and dropped the papers onto the bed.

Brady rushed to the printer and Dan crowded in beside him. Frustration gleamed in their eyes.

"One more sheet. Come on! Come on!" Brady urged.

"Done!" Dan snapped the last paper from the printer.

Brady quickly grabbed the pile of papers off the bed where Dan had slapped the final one.

"Let's go out the back way, so she doesn't see us," Dan murmured as he headed toward the doorway, where he stopped and peered out into the hallway toward the mudroom.

"Come on, hurry! They're almost here!" he hissed.

Brady quickly followed Dan; his arms laden with the papers. The two men dashed out into the hallway leaving Rafe to turn off the printer.

Tension zipped through him as he took one quick look around.

Everything appeared normal. It was like they had never just been here.

He wished he could say the same thing about the kitchen. JJ was gonna be pissed when she got back.

Hopefully not for long. Hopefully their sneaking around would have been worth it.

Rafe closed the office door and headed toward the back entrance.

A giddy excitement raged inside him as he heard JJ speaking to the baby as they entered the mud room.

Quietly, he slipped out the side door and followed Brady and Dan as they raced around to the back of the house ducking beneath windows so JJ wouldn't see them.

Man, they looked like they were on some sort of S.W.A.T. mission avoiding getting caught. But this sure was fun.

JJ frowned as she walked into the kitchen, balancing Chrissy on her hip. The dishes had been cleared from the table and piled on the counter, the soapy water was in the sink, but the dishes were still dirty.

*What in the world?*

She gazed over at the dining room table. Her dessert of apple pie had been set in the middle of the table but had been untouched. The coffee pot was full and steaming.

But no guys.

She spied a note on the kitchen counter.

*Out in the barn. Sorry, we forgot to do something urgent. Back soon.*

It was signed by Rafe.

JJ sighed and placed Chrissy back in the highchair.

"Okay, then. Looks like your daddies are back in work mode," she said to the baby who focused her gaze at the kitchen window, totally ignoring her.

A blue jay was just entering the birdfeeder there.

"I can take a hint. You want to watch the birdies," JJ said and smiled.

Good, while Christy was distracted, she would get a start on the dishes.

As she washed, she pondered on something that was beginning to make her suspicious.

The note said they had forgotten some work and were out in the barn. It was very rare they would pass up dessert, especially her apple pie. They could have eaten first and then gone. And when they volunteered to help her, they'd never backed out before.

Why volunteer so quickly to help her out and then change their minds? They *had* to be up to something. But what could it be?

A strange giggle from Chrissy made JJ gaze over at her daughter who was suddenly pounding her fists on the baby chair tray with sheer exhilaration.

"What's got you all excited, sweetie?" she asked as she returned her focus to her dishes.

Usually watching the birds kept her amused. But not this amused.

From the corner of her eye, movement at the kitchen window made JJ's head snap that way. For a moment, she could only stare in horror at the big black furry face with amber eyes that stared back at her through the screen.

A bear!

And it was a big one!

# Chapter Two

JJ stifled a scream as terror ripped through her. She didn't dare make a sound. The last thing she wanted was to startle the bear who continued to gaze in at them with fangs bared and a low, menacing growl.

Quietly and unhurriedly she lifted Chrissy out of her highchair and cursed herself for shutting off the baby monitor in the living room when she'd come back from her trip earlier. She hadn't wanted the guys to hear her crying.

Adrenalin shot through her as she carried Chrissy toward the staircase that would lead them upstairs. Even as she was thinking about going up, visions of the bear clawing its way through the screen and running after her with baby clutched in her arms, raced through her mind.

Should she go back into the living room and turn on the baby monitor and warn the guys?

She stopped at the bottom of the stairs.

Indecision raged.

If she went back and the bear climbed in, they would be trapped.

She could make a run for the barn, but if the bear didn't come inside, it would see her when she went out and chase her down and get them.

No, she had to get Christy upstairs. Hopefully, the bear wouldn't know where they'd gone. She would have to lock themselves in a room.

Panic raged as she ran up the stairs. What if the bear *did* follow them?

Chrissy must have sensed her distress, because she was deathly quiet as she stared up at JJ with wide eyes filled with uneasiness and her forehead burrowed in a frown.

Swiftly, she swept down the hall and into the nursery, quietly shutting the door. A sudden horrible thought shook her to her very core.

What if the bear had slaughtered the guys? Or if they were still alive and they came out of the barn and ran into the bear? They didn't have any weapons on them.

An unexpected eerie calmness draped over her.

Suddenly, she knew exactly what to do.

. . ⌘ . .

"DO YOU THINK SHE'LL like it?" Rafe asked.

Dan detected worry lacing Rafe's voice. From the other side of Dan, Brady laughed.

"I'm not pregnant and I like it," Brady said.

"Hopefully, it'll get us out of the doghouse for taking off on her like we did," Rafe complained.

"You mean hopefully it'll get us out of the double doghouse in us not being happy at the pregnancy news in the first place and then taking off like we did after supper without doing what we volunteered to do," Dan reminded, as he put the finishing touch on the front cover of the item they had created to surprise JJ.

"Hey, I'm happy now. It just came as a freaking surprise," Rafe replied with a frown and a shake of his head.

"Gentlemen, if we play with fire, we're gonna get burned and I don't mean it in a bad sense," Brady said with a chuckle. His blue eyes were laughing and he appeared genuinely joyful compared to earlier when they'd been given the baby news right out of the blue.

Dan smiled. Perhaps Brady thought this baby was his? He sure was a good dad to Chrissy and Dan doubted Brady would mind having more kids with JJ.

Personally, he didn't care who the dad was, as long as the kid was healthy.

"How long before we can go back inside the house?" Rafe asked.

"The gift should be dry now. We just need to wrap it," Dan answered.

He was about to reach for the item they had created for JJ, when a shot ripped through the air from the direction of the ranch house.

Shit!

"What the hell?" Brady called out as the three of them rushed out of the office and headed toward the barn door.

Dan got there first and what he saw amazed him.

JJ stood on the stairs, just outside the mudroom, rifle poised in her hand. She was aiming it eastward where three big black bears were running with lightning speed into the twilight away from the bird feeder.

"I warned her that bears like sunflower seeds," Brady chuckled from behind Dan.

"Man, she looks hot when she's protecting her homestead," Rafe muttered beneath his breath.

Dan had to agree. She did look sexy wearing that cute innocent sundress with puffy sleeves and carrying a weapon.

Suddenly, she gazed over their way, lowered the rifle and waved to them. He would have expected her to be frightened. But she appeared confident and strong.

"All in a day's work, gentlemen. Carry-on!" she shouted.

But he caught the frown on her face. Nope, she didn't look happy.

Dan swallowed as she turned and walked into the house.

"I don't know about you guys, but I get the feeling we have just entered triple doghouse hell for not being here to protect her and

Chrissy from the bears," Dan said as they hurried back into the barn office.

"Yep, she must have been scared," Brady replied with a grimace.

"We're going to have to work overtime tonight to make it up to her," Rafe said as Dan picked up the present for JJ.

"That is, if she lets us into her bed," Dan muttered, suddenly feeling dejected.

There was a reply of miserable affirmatives from Rafe and Brady.

"Come on, let's get this present wrapped and hope for the best," Brady urged.

He opened a bottom drawer of the office desk and brought out some pretty floral wrapping paper they kept for such occasions to make JJ happy with a gift. Being nowhere near a store had made them keep many items on hand...just in case.

Besides, giving her a present once in awhile always cheered her up and reminded her how much she meant to them.

He hoped it would do the same tonight.

· · ∽ · ·

JJ WAS STILL SHAKING when she put Chrissy down for the night in her crib.

In the past, the bears had not terrified her to the point of an outright panic attack. They usually didn't come around, but there had been occasions when they'd raided the birdfeeder. Most of the time she remembered to make sure it was empty before nightfall.

But she'd been busy today and it hadn't even occurred to her to check. The earlier blue jay at the birdfeeder should have been a clue.

JJ shook her head at overlooking that chore and gently covered her daughter with a blanket. She was already fast asleep.

There were so many times that she would study her baby and wonder what if there was some medical emergency and Chrissy got deathly ill. Or what if something happened to her and her daughter would have to grow up without a mother.

The nearest hospital was hours away with the plane.

Her anxiety should have been somewhat alleviated to learn that a young bush doctor had taken up residence a few lakes away at some secluded cabin.

She hadn't met the man yet, but her friend and nearest neighbour, Milena Allen, had met him earlier this spring when Milena and the men over at Snowy Creek Ranch had a run in with some poachers and Milena had been shot.

The police, plus a wildlife expert and the new doctor had shown up within a couple of hours of the incident. But JJ knew if Milena's injury had been worse, the delay could have meant her life.

JJ shivered at the thought of losing Milena. The woman had spent years in prison just like herself, and she hadn't become bitter behind bars. If anything, being incarcerated and then suddenly being free, had made both of them value everything outside of prison bars.

She even appreciated the lives of the black bears that had come to visit. They were hungry and looking for food.

Now that the incident was over and she'd calmed somewhat, she remembered the eerie calm that had come over her as she'd grabbed Dan's rifle from where he kept it high in his closet. Hurriedly placed in the bullets and then she'd left her daughter in her crib, and crept downstairs. The bear hadn't broken in as her imagination had conjured. Instead it had remained by the birdfeeder.

She'd gone out the mudroom door and then fired a shot over the bear's head. She'd been surprised when two more black bears had suddenly appeared and followed the one who'd been raiding the birdfeeder.

Her first instinct had been to shoot the animals dead. Something inside of her, an overwhelming instinct to protect her baby, had kicked in and she'd almost gone batshit crazy, but she'd reined in her impulse to kill.

Thankfully all the excitement had tired out Chrissy. If all went good, her daughter would sleep through the night.

She smiled when she heard the guys come in. Heard them talking quietly downstairs.

Normally she'd go down and join in on their talk of the ranch, but she was quite satisfied to stand right here and gaze down at her sleeping daughter.

They had gotten Chrissy into a well-rounded routine. She slept up to eleven hours straight through the night now and awoke bright-eyed and happy.

It hadn't been that way the first few months. She'd awoken every couple of hours and thankfully the guys had taken turns feeding her and caring for her during the night, allowing JJ to sleep.

She was so lucky to have these three men in her life.

They loved her; it was so easy for her to see.

Love sparkled in their eyes when they looked at her. They went out of their way to make sure she had their help with the daily workload. They pleasured her when she wanted that kind of attention and she knew when they wanted sex too.

She could read each of her men like a book. Which made her wonder what they were up to tonight?

Ordinarily they would have come running to ask is she was okay after she'd fired the shot. They hadn't.

She frowned. It was too quiet.

Yep, they were definitely up to something.

But finding out what it was would just have to wait because she needed a nice hot shower and then she wanted all her cowboys in her bed tonight.

And she wanted them really bad.

*Damn hormones.*

Reluctantly, she left the nursery. As she stepped into the hallway, she met Dan, who, it appeared, had been waiting for her.

He grinned and her insides went electric at that sexy smile.

"Hey, baby mama. You look really sexy shooting a rifle. You're the most beautiful pregnant woman and we hope you'll forgive us for taking off on you. But we think it was worth it. We hope you do too."

JJ shivered with excitement as Dan took her by the hand and led her across the hallway.

When she entered her bedroom, she was surprised to find Brady and Rafe standing beside her bed.

They looked sheepish when they saw her and then she followed their gaze to her bed, where she saw a gift wrapped present.

She giggled as happiness raced through her.

"I knew it. I knew you guys were up to something," she gushed.

"Sorry, baby. We didn't mean to cut out on you, but we just wanted you to have this tonight. We were just surprised at the news. But we all welcome a baby," Brady said in a serious tone.

Relief splashed through JJ at Brady's confession.

"It's for you and the newbie," Rafe added.

"Come on, open it up," Dan pushed.

Her three men smiled at her and she wondered why she would ever have thought they would be upset at the baby news.

Wonderful emotions of giddiness and excitement clutched at her chest as she sat on the edge of her bed and unwrapped the present.

Her heart sang with extreme happiness as she gazed at the gift.

"You made this?" she asked them as she ran her fingers over a white felt-covered binder. There were cute flowers and homemade cut-out felt cowboy hats on the cover.

"Yeah," Brady replied. He had such a sweet grin on his face that she swore she fell in love with him all over again.

"One is light brown, one black, one white, for each of us guys," Brady explained as he pointed out each cowboy hat.

"The pretty bright yellow felt flower is you," Dan chimed in.

"The pink flower is Chrissy and the light yellow one is for the newbie," Rafe added.

Newbie? JJ smiled. They already had a nickname for her baby.

"Open it," Dan instructed.

JJ did as he directed.

*Your first visit to the doctor* was printed on the top of the first page. That would be today.

"It's a pregnancy journal," Dan explained.

"I can see that," she answered. She wanted to say more, but emotions were welling inside of her chest.

She began flipping through the colorful pages.

There was one sheet that had the words along the top: *feelings when you discovered you were pregnant.*

Well, she had been shocked.

Yet another page that said: *morning sickness.* And more: *happy days, sad days, weight gain, first ultrasound, baby name ideas, birth plans.*

She stopped flipping as reality set in.

"I need to contact Layla."

"You're going with the midwife again?" Rafe asked.

He didn't sound too happy.

"You don't want to have the baby in a hospital setting?" Brady asked in a much too hopeful voice.

"Won't it be safer in the city?" Dan asked.

JJ frowned and gazed at her concerned cowboys.

"Hey, I'm the one who is supposed to be the scaredy cat. Not you guys. Why the glum faces? Yes, we are going with the midwife. I don't want to take anyone away from the ranch. I want you all with me again. Besides, Layla did a wonderful job delivering Chrissy, and you guys did a great job too. I feel like I and the baby are in safe hands with my team."

It appeared the men were at a loss for words as they stared back at her. Them not knowing what to say was rare.

A surge of self-assurance flooded her and it made her feel good. She would be fully in charge this time around. She'd already been through this once. She knew what to expect. She would be a pro.

She returned her attention to the pregnancy journal.

Yes, she was going to enjoy writing down everything.

*Your plans for the nursery...*

Goodness, where would they put the new baby? They'd think of something. There was so much room in this ranch house.

She stopped at the next page.

"This is my favorite page," she whispered.

She shivered with delight as the guys peered down at the title she pointed to.

*Pregnancy Cravings.*

Their breaths came faster as they caught her meaning. During her last pregnancy, her hormones had her craving sex. Big time!

"Why don't you freshen up. We'll meet you in the room in twenty minutes," Rafe said. His voice sounded hoarse and thick with arousal.

*The room.*

It was at the end of the hall and where they all went during their foursome nights. It had the king-sized bed.

Her breaths quickened and her body tightened with exquisite tension.

JJ nodded.

She laughed when Brady suddenly raced for the door.

First one downstairs gets that shower!" he called out.

Rafe and Dan chased after him.

There were a couple of other bathrooms with showers up here down the hall, so she knew the guys were just playing with Brady.

There were some amused shouts downstairs and then silence.

JJ waited a few moments, listening for Chrissy. Thankfully, she hadn't been disturbed. She would be used to the noise of the guys by now. They were a cheerful, loud bunch and she loved all of them with her whole heart.

She was glad too that Brady could run again.

He barely limped now after that horrific tetanus scare last year. And Rafe had fully recovered after slicing his leg open by accidentally chopping into it with an axe when he'd been surprised by a couple of wolves at a cabin he'd been staying at while checking cattle.

At those frightening memories, that niggle of anxiety zipped back, pushing away her happiness about the pregnancy journal. The binder was a good start in alleviating her fears that they might not like the idea of another baby on the way, but she was still worried, her mind filled with the dreadful what if this happens and what if that happens scenarios.

She forced herself to inhale a deep breath, counted to four and then exhaled slowly. And what had she been thinking about having this baby out here at the ranch with a midwife again?

The midwife had barely made it in time last winter due to high winds and a storm. The guys had done their best in trying to keep her calm, but she'd been terrified during labor.

Her earlier confidence vanished.

There would be pain. Maybe something would go wrong? What if something happened to the baby? Or to her?

She shivered at those thoughts and then forced herself to slow her racing thoughts before they went out of control and she flew into a full-blown panic attack. Now was not the time to lose it. Not with a pleasure-filled evening with her three cowboys awaiting her.

She realized the only reason she'd been reacting this way was because she was tired from a long day and plenty of surprises.

The baby news. The guys not so enthusiastic reaction. The bears and her almost going bat shit crazy with the rifle on those poor animals.

She blew out a tense breath. She'd feel better when all her men were in bed with her.

With that thought squarely in place, she settled the beautiful pregnancy journal onto her desk, resisting the urge to flip through it some more.

Instead, she gazed out the nearby slightly open window.

Her window looked out across their vegetable garden behind the house and the spooky black forest beyond. Tonight, the half full moon shone like a candle illuminating the cages Dan had made with chicken wire to cover their plants so the deer, bears and other animals couldn't stomp on them or start chewing on the leaves.

The breeze was cold and brisker than earlier when she and Chrissy had been down at the lake and the wind breathed a chill through her. She reached up to close the window and stopped when the hoot of an owl drifted into the room.

It sounded close. Probably at the edge of the forest. It was most likely waiting for a mouse or a mole to scamper through the garden so it could fly down, swoop it up and dine on the defenseless victim.

And then she heard the spine-tingling howl of wolves far off. The animals were probably checking out the cattle in the various pastures interspersed throughout the woods.

She remembered their earlier conversation at dinner tonight. Brady and Dan had been talking about the wolf trouble and Rafe had been staring at her, deep in thought, with an odd expression on his face.

She hadn't liked that look. As if he'd been frightened of something.

Was he afraid he might be the baby's father? Oh, she hoped that wasn't it. She would have to question him about what he'd been thinking so deeply that Brady and Dan had had to say his name several times before he'd come out of his weird trance.

She knew that having a baby with Rafe would be something special. Just like it had been with Brady. So, she hoped he wasn't afraid to become a dad, especially if this baby was his.

She dreamed of having at least one baby fathered by each of her cowboys. Three children. Wouldn't that be something?

While in prison, she would occasionally wonder what her life would have been like had she never been incarcerated. Her thoughts had always centered on one man for a husband, a nice house with a big backyard, a couple of kids, maybe a dog and a cat.

But never had she ever imagined living in a ranch house and having sex with three hot men. Her pussy and behind clenched with a demanding need for pleasure as visions of what would be happening tonight suddenly danced in her head.

She blew out an aroused breath.

Whew, suddenly she was feeling very hot and bothered.

Time to head for her shower.

Time for a little bit of fun.

Brady quietly stepped into JJ's bedroom and listened to the running water coming from her bathroom.

Good. She was still in the shower. He wanted to snuggle with her before they met up with Dan and Rafe.

He opened the bathroom door and inhaled as the warm mist enveloped his face. Quietly, he closed the door behind him, dropped the towel he'd slung around his waist and for a moment watched her shadow on the other side of the glass door.

His heart clenched.

Even with the mist shrouding the bevelled glass, he could see her arms were uplifted. She was washing her hair and she was the most beautiful woman in the world.

How had he gotten so lucky in having JJ in his life? There were many times he asked himself that question. Mainly because so many things could have gone differently and the two of them would never have met.

After killing her stepfather, she could have had better lawyers. They could have prevented her from going to prison in the first place. Prevented her from coming here.

If he'd never quit Toronto and stayed in the city, he would never have come out here.

His sister, Jenna, who ran Cowboys Online, a program that helped convicts get out of prison earlier, might have picked another person. They had requested a man or two to help around the ranch. Had Jenna obeyed their request, men would have come instead of JJ.

Brady bit his bottom lip to prevent himself from swearing out loud at how many other things could have prevented them from getting together.

Her mother not dying. His parents not dying. Jenna not starting her Cowboys online program.

He gave himself a mental shake. He needed to stay in the present and not think about what if this had happened or had not happened. Sometimes he had to fight those what if thoughts.

He could not think about a life without JJ. He couldn't. He wouldn't.

He needed to stay in the present and thank God that He had sent her to them and sent this new baby on the way. It didn't matter who the father was. This baby would be his. All of theirs.

Brady nodded confidently to himself and then slid open the glass shower door.

She was rinsing her hair, but she spied him immediately.

Her eyes darkened with desire and her face transformed from one of worry to one of extreme happiness. For a split second, he wondered why she had been worrying, but that thought disappeared as she held out her arms to him.

Excitement and arousal swept through him as he stepped into the shower and he curled his arms around her, hugging her tight to his body.

She hugged him back.

"What took you so long?" she whispered against his ear.

"I bet you say that to all the guys," he chuckled.

# Chapter Three

She laughed, nuzzled her face into Brady's shoulder and wrapped her warm arms around his waist.

He inhaled as she pushed her breasts against his chest and then she pressed against him with the rest of her body. In response, his stiff cock nudged intimately against her lower abdomen.

They stood that way, melded against one another for a couple of minutes, neither saying anything as the hot water sluiced over them.

He sensed she needed this closeness and he realized they *had* taken her for granted today. They had hurt her feelings in not reacting appropriately concerning the surprise pregnancy or in not checking in on her after she'd shot at the bears.

Why had they acted so cold toward the baby news? The only answer he could come up with was they'd been in shock.

Yes, he'd dreamed of having another baby with JJ, just not yet. But she was having one. They all were having another baby. How cool was that?

Her skin was so soft and silky as he slid his hands off her warm back and moved his palms slowly down her sides and caressed over her hips, memorizing every delicious curve, while inhaling deeply.

He could smell her arousal. Musky and intoxicating.

Her scent always did something wickedly delicious to him. Made him very aware of her. Made him primal.

But he put a strong hold on his needs as he slipped his hands between their bodies and placed his palms over her baby bump.

Yeah, he could feel she was pregnant. Or was that just his imagination? Was this *his* baby? Or was it Rafe's or Dan's?

Why wasn't he jealous of the idea that this baby might not be his?

Instincts told him Dan and Rafe would be perfect dads. Just like they were to Chrissy. There was nothing to be jealous about, but still, a part of him hoped this kid belonged to him, just like Chrissy did.

"How did I miss this? Not knowing you're pregnant?" he growled above the spray of the shower, feeling a bit pissed.

He should have known.

"I didn't notice it either," she replied.

She gazed down and slipped her warm hands possessively over his.

"I missed you all day," he confessed.

"I missed you too," she replied, her lips upturned in a stunning smile.

"Why don't we pick up where we left off in the kitchen just before supper? Maybe a little quickie before the guys have their way with me?" she teased.

Alertness rocked him as she stood on her tippy toes and then she gently sucked his left earlobe into her mouth. He felt his cock harden even more against her.

He trembled as shivers of excitement coursed through him. He couldn't wait to be with her tonight.

He heard her inhale softly as she felt him throb against her lower abdomen.

Despite his eagerness for sex, he needed to apologize to her.

"Man, I am really sorry about today. Can you ever forgive me for not being happy right from the start? I mean, I am happy and I should have showed you—"

She stopped nibbling on his earlobe, lifted her head away and her brown eyes shone with so much love, the power of that look just about brought him to his knees.

"Nothing to forgive, Brady. You guys more than made up for it with the thoughtful gift. I am going to enjoy writing in that baby journal."

Brady shook his head.

"No, we can't be forgiven because we give you gifts. That's just not right."

She tenderly sucked on her bottom lip, as if suddenly deep in thought.

Man, she looked sexy with that pensive look.

"Hmm, maybe you're right," she said.

His gut clenched. So, she *did* think they were assholes. That thought hurt, and it should.

"Don't look so devastated, Brady. I can find all kinds of ways for all of you to make it up to me."

She beamed and he relaxed and moved his hips harder against her, trapping his cock between their bodies.

"I like the way you think," he growled.

Just then he noticed shadows on the other side of the shower glass.

Sons of bitches.

"They're here," he muttered.

"I know," she giggled. She reached behind him and turned off the taps.

"About time you two got out of there. We want our woman," Rafe growled as Brady slid the door open.

Rafe and Dan stood there, towels slung low over their hips, their hair damp from their own showers.

Brady held out his hand to JJ. She took it and blushed prettily as she stepped out of the shower.

Yeah, a pregnancy glow. She had that.

She did look different. Brighter. So beautiful.

Rafe and Dan's gazes grew darker as they studied her nakedness. They were probably checking to see if she had a baby bump, just like he'd been doing.

Having her pregnant again, well, it was suddenly turning him on so much, he wasn't sure if he could make it to the other room without pushing her up against the wall and taking her.

He blew out a tense breath as Rafe grabbed a towel and wrapped it around her. Then Dan grabbed another towel and began to dry her hair.

"Now this is what I call service," she said in a low aroused voice.

"Please, our Queen, forgive us for our sins," Dan said seductively as he slid the towel off her hair and then leaned over and began rubbing along her inner thighs toward the juncture between her legs.

Brady couldn't help but let out a laugh.

"So, this is what it's all about. You two want to get into her good graces," Brady commented as he held a hand to his chest with a shocked expression on his face.

Dan chuckled.

"And you weren't by stepping into the shower with her?" Rafe answered with a wink.

"Caught red-handed," Brady quipped as he grabbed a towel from the nearby shelf and quickly dried himself.

He watched as JJ's facial expression turn from appreciation to one of sensuality as the men continued their naughty ministrations.

With the men towel drying her, joking with each other and watching her with exquisite need flaring in their eyes, fevered heat slashed through JJ.

She struggled to breathe as they delicately touched her intimate areas.

Brady's gaze captured her attention. His blue eyes were bright with excitement and stormy with lust. Her breathing went faster and she cried out as he grabbed her by her hand and pulled her away from the guys and their seductive towel touches.

"Hey! She's not dry yet!" Rafe protested.

"We don't want her dry!" Brady growled.

From behind her, she heard both Rafe and Dan swear softly as they caught Brady's meaning.

"I would have lost it and taken you right there, if they'd kept touching you like that," Brady muttered as he picked up speed, moving them down the hallway.

Despite her arousal, JJ couldn't help but giggle. She loved that she had so much sexual power over Brady. Just thinking about her sensual claim on her cowboys and what they wanted to do with her tonight, made her breasts swell and her nipples ache to have their mouths sucking on her. A spike of hot cream gushed down her vagina at those thoughts.

Brady drew her into the darkened bedroom and stopped just inside the doorway. He let go of her hand and pushed her gently up against the wall. Then he moved against her and she inhaled as his large erection pressed hot and heavy against her abdomen.

"I should take you right here and now," he growled.

"Then, do it," she teased, her voice thick with excitement.

From the hallway, light splashed over his face. She spied that his smile was tight and full of promise.

"I'll let the others have their way with you first," he murmured.

He lowered his head and she felt the intoxicating brush of his chest against her ultra tender nipples.

She expected a kiss, but he teased her lips ever so softly with a brush of his mouth and before she could respond, he stepped away as Dan and Rafe entered the room.

Rafe took Brady's place in front of her. His gaze was smouldering and seductive, his body heat making her moan. She felt his heavy erection push against her left thigh.

"Let's get you some pleasure," Rafe purred.

His face lowered and his lips kissed the length of her throat, sparking blades of fire. She moaned at the intoxicating touches of his mouth as his warm lips moved over her flesh. She hissed as he kissed lower, across her chest, stopping at her left breast. Then his mouth sucked her nipple into his hot cavern.

She could barely keep her eyes open as he nibbled on her tender bud, creating an insane friction with his raspy tongue.

She spied Dan nudging in beside Rafe. Dan's head drew downward. His lips parted as he drew her other nipple into his mouth.

Fiery sensations shimmered and blossomed through her as both men suckled her nipples. Her breasts felt huge as they cupped her mounds into their calloused palms and squeezed gently.

In response, her pussy quivered and dropped with need.

She moaned and reached out, slapping her hands upon their bare muscular backs, holding herself steady as their lips worked their magic, drawing on her flesh and sucking.

She gave out a broken cry as Brady's calloused fingers roughly massaged her clitoris, bringing her quickly to the edge of the ecstasy she craved.

He slipped a finger into her vagina, and her wet muscles clenched around him like a vice.

"Oh, baby, you really are hot, tonight," Brady growled.

She felt heady. Wanted to respond to what he'd said, but no words came to mind. She'd already slipped into the pleasure they created, gyrating her hips as she anticipated the climax that was quickly building.

Brady slid two fingers into her.

She felt her entire body tightening. She dug her fingers into their backs.

Brady withdrew.

Frustration clawed through her. She shuddered as he thrust three fingers into her sopping vagina, his digits caressing her throbbing vaginal walls.

Yes!

She clenched her teeth, bucked against all three of them as she craved a harder flesh to flesh contact. They were controlling her passions, and it was exasperating as heck!

"She's ready," came Brady's low hiss.

Suddenly she was being moved away from the wall, into a new position. She didn't know what was happening, or where in the room they'd taken her, but suddenly her arms were being lifted and she felt the warm fur of the bondage cuffs around her wrists.

*Ah, that's why the lights had been out, so they could surprise her with the rope hanging from the eyelet in the ceiling.*

JJ closed her eyes as the ache to be filled claimed her vagina and her ass. Someone moved in front of her, she could feel their body heat. She struggled to open her heavy-lidded eyes and saw Brady there. His head lowered and he kissed her full on the mouth, sending her senses spiralling.

Her lips felt bruised as a few seconds later, he pulled his head away.

Moonlight splashed over his face and she noticed his cheeks were flushed with excitement.

"Hey, baby, are you ready for some hot love?"

JJ nodded jerkily and creamed with anticipation. Somewhere behind her came the rip of plastic as someone accessed a condom.

And then JJ heard the slurp of lube.

JJ cried out as someone eased in behind her.

Who was it? Rafe? Dan?

Strong, calloused hands clenched at her waist, holding her steady.

Suddenly, from in front of her, Brady's possessive mouth covered hers, short circuiting her brain and vanquishing all coherent thoughts. His tongue entered her mouth and mated with hers until her pussy was quivering and the rest of her was drowning in red-hot flames of need.

Then, he pressed his shaft into her wet vagina, his broad cockhead parting her soft labia folds. She mewed at the fullness of his penetration and arched against him, enjoying the sensuality he created.

Then he withdrew and powered into her again. He began a slow, delightful thrust that spun pleasure through her like a spider's web, capturing her and holding her within its tantalizing grip.

Heat touched her back as someone leaned against her. Strong hands cradled her hips. A thick, lubed cockhead pushed against her tight sphincter and then hesitated. Her ass automatically clenched, protesting any intrusion.

Rafe. It had to be him. She could hear his soft inhalations and she could feel the hard contours of his chest muscles as he pressed himself against her from behind.

Brady withdrew.

And then Rafe's solid penis stretched into her, entering in a quick thrust that had her gasping into Brady's mouth as a succulent pinch of pain rocked through her. Her anal muscles parted and greedily gripped Rafe's cock.

He groaned his approval.

Yes, Rafe. He was exactly what she needed right now. Rough and hard. But she sensed he was holding back his force and she knew it was because of the baby.

She smiled inwardly. The baby would be fine during sexual relations for the time being, the doctor had said. She'd have to have a talk with the guys about not being too afraid.

But, sweet heavens, not now!

Rafe withdrew and Brady's shaft entered her again. Her vaginal muscles welcomed him in a tightening embrace. Then he withdrew and Rafe's hot erection entered her quivering anus.

She jerked between them as blades of pressure and pleasure built inside of her.

The men began pistoning in a steady, quick pace. Sometimes one at a time. Sometimes both together.

Her body tightened.

Perspiration blossomed over her skin as she strained beneath the incredible tension they were creating. Fiery heat curled through her, lapping at her every intimate muscle.

Her juices were flowing now. Hot and lubricating. She was almost ready. Almost there.

Brady growled like a wild animal and tore his mouth from hers. He fervently kissed her neck and caressed her throat with his tongue. His breaths were rough and she sensed he was nearing his climax.

Behind her, Rafe's breaths grew faster and heavier. His pistoning drives became urgent.

Both men bucked against her, and JJ gasped for air as fever heat lanced her. Her body was ultra-sensitive to their every touch, to their every lightning speed thrust. Every stroke into her pushed her closer to the flames of pleasure.

And then she shattered and entered a brilliant world of pleasure.

Convulsions consumed her. She thrashed and shuddered and drowned inside the violent spasms that rocked through her. She keened and Brady's mouth clamped over hers, muffling her, as she danced and writhed like a maniacal puppet imprisoned between the two male bodies.

Her arched arms tugged against her restraints. Her hips jerked as the carnal explosions raged.

The insane pleasure whipped her into such a frenzy, she barely registered Rafe's sensual cries as he came inside her. She hardly heard Brady as he groaned and convulsed within his own orgasm. They bucked and pushed and thrust into her, all of them enjoying the vortex.

And then all too soon, the pleasure spasms ebbed away.

Afterwards, the two men stayed buried inside of her. Their breaths slowing, an occasional jerk of one or the other's cock inside her trembling body as she stood sandwiched between their muscular bodies.

This is exactly what I needed, she thought. She felt fantastic in her after sex glow. Reborn. So relaxed and happy.

"My turn. Hey, guys. I'm dying here," came Dan's thick voice from somewhere behind Brady. Brady muttered something unintelligible as he slowly withdrew. Rafe quickly followed.

"You're all mine, sweet baby mamma," Dan whispered against her ear as he reached up and released the cuffs from her wrists.

She curled her arms around his neck and drew his head closer. His strong hands cupped her ass cheeks and he squeezed as he pulled her against his hard length.

Despite just having had a wonderful orgasm, she wanted another one. This time from Dan.

"Make love to me," she purred, loving the way Dan's eyes twinkled at her command.

He kissed her mouth as if her lips were delicate petals of a flower. His stiff cockhead boldly pushed against her ultra sensitive clitoris and he began to massage her there, quickly creating the need for more pleasure.

His mouth slanted harder over hers. She opened and his tongue darted inside tangling with hers.

She tilted her hips, craving more pressure on her clitoris. She whimpered her need and Dan moved his cockhead harder against her. She loved the incredible way her vaginal muscles were clenching, awaiting his penetration.

He groaned as she wantonly gyrated against him. Then she arched and cried into his mouth as he thrust his thick shaft deep into her, sliding past her already sensitive, wet muscles, which eagerly clenched the erotic intrusion, and drove shuttering sensations through her.

Dan's thrusts became faster, stronger, as he powered into her. Her thighs tightened and she kissed him harder, brushing her nipples against his hot chest generating an awesome friction.

She felt hands on her body. Knew they were Brady and Rafe touching her, stroking her arms, her back, making love to her flesh with their work-roughened hands.

Dan plunged into her over and over until she was gasping into his mouth as erotic tremors grabbed hold and spun through her, catapulting her toward another orgasm.

Her legs tensed, and her stomach clenched and then she shattered. Pure pleasure grabbed hold and once again she lost all control as she bucked and writhed against Dan and the hands that made love to her. She twisted and keened as her entire being was swept away by the consuming flames that twirled her into a storm-tossed world that only consisted of her cowboys and an incredible whirlwind of pleasure.

Oh mercy, they sure were making it up to her for being such bad cowboys today, yes siree.

. . ◦◦◦ . .

BRADY WAS DREAMING about how they'd taken JJ last night. Dreaming of her sexy moans after they'd cuffed her and he and Rafe had then double penetrated her followed by Dan. Her erotic sounds had made him glad they'd brought her immense pleasure at the end of a day where they'd caused her such sorrow.

Tonight, was his night to be with her. His alone time with her. He would make sure she was pleasured so much that she forgot about him being such an asshole where the baby was concerned. He smiled as he thought of the baby. No matter who the father was, he would love the baby because it was a part of JJ.

It was the insistent ringing of the landline telephone beside the bed that rocked Brady out of his hot dreams. He opened his eyes to darkness and felt disoriented as he tried to find the telephone before the shrill of it woke everyone up.

Finally, he found it and picked up the receiver.

"Moose Ranch," he mumbled automatically.

There came a silence and for a moment he figured it was some sort of marketing call or just a phantom call they sometimes received with no one on the other end.

He was just about to hang up when a sob caught his full attention.

"Brady?" came a familiar woman's voice. He instantly made out the tremor in her voice and knew something was very wrong.

It was Jenna. His sister.

His entire body tensed. Instincts told him it most likely had to do with her husband, Tim, who she'd caught stepping outside of the marriage on a couple of occasions. That he'd had affairs had totally devasted her. But she'd taken him back. Had stuck by the bastard. Heaven only knew why.

"Jenna? What is it? Are you alright?"

"It's Tim," came her meek voice.

He knew it!

Protective rage filled him and he clutched the receiver so hard, he swore he heard it crack.

"What did Tim do, Jenna?" *That son of a bitch. I'm going to kill him.*

"He's...oh, God. He's dead. Tim's dead."

"Are you kidding me?" he blurted. Even as he said those words, he kicked himself. Of course she wasn't kidding. But what she'd just said wasn't sinking in.

"The funeral is tomorrow."

Her words felt like a bucket of ice-cold water being dumped on his head. He began to shiver and he swore.

"What is it? What's wrong?" came JJ's sleepy voice from beside him.

"It's Jenna," Brady explained.

He returned his attention to his sister who was now sobbing even more. His heart clenched with sorrow for her.

*Shit. Tim dead.*

"What happened?" he asked her.

"Can you come?" she asked between sobs.

Brady nodded. "I can come. Not a problem. I can leave this morning."

"And Mitch? Can you bring him too?" Her request was followed by a hiccup.

"I can grab him on my way. Where are you?"

As Jenna told him her whereabouts, the light on the other side of the bed switched on, illuminating the bedroom. As he stared at the dark window, listening to Jenna, he could hear Dan and Rafe were now awake and quietly speaking to JJ in the background asking her what was happening.

Brady inhaled his sorrow and took solace in JJ's hand as it curled over his left shoulder like a hot, comforting brand.

"What's wrong?" JJ asked.

"Tim's dead," he whispered to her.

JJ gasped and he heard Rafe and Dan curse softly. He wished he hadn't just come right out and said it. Although JJ had never met Tim, Brady knew she would be heartbroken for Jenna.

Jenna started full out crying and he couldn't understand what she was saying. Something about cancer and a week to live. Frustration made him thrust the phone at JJ.

"Can you try to calm her down? I need to get dressed. We need to get out of here at first light and pick up Mitch. Jenna's a mess."

JJ nodded. Her face was white with anxiety as she grabbed the phone and started to speak.

Tim was dead? He hadn't liked the guy since finding out he was a two-timer, but he hadn't wished the guy death. What the hell had happened to Tim? Was Brady really awake? Maybe he was having a nightmare?

Pain and tremors shot through both Brady's legs as he swung them out of bed and sat up. He took a moment to get his bearings and waited for the shaking in his legs to subside. That tetanus he'd wrangled with awhile back sometimes reared its ugly head, like this morning.

From behind him he could hear JJ's calming questions as she spoke with Jenna. Heard the comforters' rustle as the guys got out of bed on the other side. He quickly gazed at the windup clock on the night table and ran his hand over his stubbled chin.

Four forty-five. It would be light enough to fly soon. He stood and chills rocked through him. He needed to get dressed.

"What happened to Tim?" Rafe asked as he met Brady at the door.

"She said something about cancer. Didn't even know he was sick," Brady answered. He felt like a zombie. The bad news hadn't sunk in yet.

# Chapter Four

B eside him, Rafe swore.

"I need to grab a quick shower and get dressed. I need to contact my brother," Brady said.

"I'll see if I can contact, Mitch. But I doubt it. They have lousy cell service unless they're up on that hill," Rafe reminded him.

Brady nodded. Shoot, he'd totally forgotten about that.

"I'll get the coffee on first. That'll clear your cobwebs. I'll start breakfast too and try to contact Mitch," Rafe said and then he rushed down the hallway.

Brady noticed Rafe had already thrown on his clothes from yesterday.

"Hey, man. Are you okay? You look like shit," Dan muttered as he joined him at the bedroom doorway. He too was already dressed in yesterday's clothing.

"I always look like shit," Brady replied with a chuckle. Leave it to Dan to cheer him up, even with a death.

"Here, fresh underwear," Dan thrust the garment into Brady's trembling hands.

Brady quickly donned the underwear.

"I'll throw some clothes and toothbrush and stuff into a bag for you. Don't worry about the ranch, we can handle things. You go take a shower," Dan said with a reassuring smile and rushed away.

Man, this was crazy. Tim was dead.

Brady gazed back at JJ, who was clutching the receiver. Her knuckles were white as she spoke softly to Jenna. Why had he given JJ the task of calming Jenna down? When he'd heard Jenna start to cry, he'd just lost it, that's why.

His oldest sister was the strongest person he knew. She never cried. Even when they'd almost lost their youngest sister, Ginny, and when their parents had died. Just thinking of his parents and the fast way they'd been torn out of all their lives had Brady moving into the hallway toward the nursery.

Suddenly he needed to see his baby daughter. Needed to see that she was okay. Silently, he slipped into her room and left the door open allowing the hall light to spill onto her crib.

She was fast asleep and smiling, totally oblivious of the unfolding chaos around her.

Brady's gut clenched and his heart filled with happiness at the beautiful sight. Last night, JJ had dressed her in a yellow fleece sleeper outfit and a matching yellow fleece hat to keep her head warm. Man, she was the most beautiful little girl he'd ever seen in his life. He was so glad he'd survived that tetanus scare and lived to see his daughter get born and blossom into such a pretty little thing.

He didn't know how long he stood there staring down at her, feeling immense love flow through him, but a gentle hand at his waist tore him from his trance.

JJ moved against him and he relished the warmth from her body.

"I'll grab some coffee and then head down to the lake to get the plane ready and send in my flight plan. We can take off in less than an hour," she whispered. She was already dressed and he wondered how long he'd been standing here admiring his little girl.

He didn't know what was wrong with him. Usually he was so strong under strenuous situations but this news about Tim's death had just floored him.

Truth was, he didn't want to leave Moose Ranch. Didn't want to go and face death. Face Tim's funeral and then try to figure out how to help Jenna. He needed to stay here with JJ and his baby and the baby on the way. Stay here where it was safe. Hell, the plane could go down on the way to the airport and Chrissy would be an orphan.

For a moment an incredible burst of emotion crashed over him and he almost decided to refuse to go, but the moment passed. He couldn't be selfish. His sister needed him. She'd always been there for him and now it was time to pay her back. It was time to leave Moose Ranch.

。。 ⌒⌒ 。。

THE NEXT FEW HOURS had been a whirlwind. Dan was sticking close to the ranch for the day doing only the necessities. Rafe had volunteered to take care of Chrissy until JJ could return.

At first light, JJ had flown Brady over to Snowy Creek Ranch, where Brady had broken the news to his brother as they hadn't been able to reach him by phone. Mitch had been stunned and had agreed to go with Brady to the funeral and to help their sister through this crisis.

Mitch's partners had hurriedly packed a suitcase and lunch for Mitch. Milena had immediately retrieved two all-terrain vehicles so they could drive back to the lake as they'd had to walk in from the plane.

Within half an hour they'd been back in the air. JJ had flown the two somber brothers to a private Thunder Bay airfield that included a lake for float planes to land. There they'd managed to charter a flight to Toronto where Tim's body lay in a funeral home. Their youngest sister, Ginny, would meet Brady and Mitch. But first, they'd have to wait a few hours for the charter to arrive as it was out on another job. Brady had insisted she go back home and not wait with them.

On the phone, Jenna had told JJ that Tim had started feeling unwell about three weeks ago. They'd figured he'd picked up a virus that was going around. But then two weeks ago, he'd started coughing and hadn't been able to stop.

Jenna had brought him to a rural clinic run by a nurse practitioner. An X ray discovered something suspicious in both his lungs. Because

Tim's breathing was failing, they'd airlifted him to a hospital in Sault Ste. Marie where a subsequent Cat Scan revealed masses in both of his lungs. He'd been sent to a cancer specialty hospital in Toronto where an emergency biopsy had been done on each of his lungs. The news hadn't been promising.

Jenna had said they'd opened Tim up for exploratory surgery a couple of days ago and quickly closed. The cancer was in both lungs and had spread to the surrounding lymph nodes and beyond. They had given him no hope. Had told them he might have six weeks to live.

He'd died last night. He'd been a heavy smoker when he'd been younger, Jenna had confessed. But he hadn't had a cigarette since they'd been together.

It happened so fast, Jenna had said. Too fast. She hadn't even been able to say goodbye to him.

*It happened so fast.* Jenna's words rolled around in JJ's head like a volley of bullets.

She could lose Rafe, Dan or Brady, just like that. Or Chrissy. Or her unborn baby. Mentally, she pictured herself snapping her fingers. Gone. Just like that.

Chills shot through JJ as she imagined what Jenna must have been going through the last three weeks. Not knowing that at the end of it, her husband would be dead.

Oh, dear Lord. Poor Jenna.

What if the same thing happened to JJ? What if the plane Brady and Mitch were on crashed? What if Dan and Rafe worked so hard this week while Brady was away that one of them had a heart attack and dropped dead? What if Chrissy got a serious illness and couldn't be cured? What if JJ lost the baby?

Suddenly the cockpit windshield seemed to waver. The plane's walls appeared to move in toward her. Her heart began to race. Creepy shivers raced up her spine and crawled all over her skull.

Nervousness snapped through her like a live wire.

*Oh, crap! Calm down!*

JJ inhaled deeply and tried to concentrate on the scenery below. The patchwork of green trees and the wildflower filled meadows and the shimmering blue lakes. But nothing looked nice. Everything felt so wrong.

She couldn't breathe right. She needed to get out of here. She *had* to land the plane.

Perspiration blossomed across her forehead and her breaths came faster and faster. Her lips began to tingle.

*Oh God! No! Not now!*

She was starting to hyperventilate. She needed a paper bag to breathe into or she'd soon start to feel lightheaded. She was inhaling too much oxygen. She knew there was a very small possibility that she could pass out. Although, she'd never lost consciousness, she didn't want to chance it happening up here in the plane.

*No!* Now, her fingers were beginning to tingle.

JJ scanned the cockpit. There was nothing she could use to breathe into!

*Calm down! Just land the plane! You will be safe once you land the plane!*

She nodded jerkily.

She just needed to find a big lake. And just like that a decent sized lake appeared on the horizon. She angled the plane toward it.

JJ inhaled into the paper bag that she'd found crumpled on one of the back seats and thankfully the bag had no holes in it. Making sure to cover her nose and mouth with the opening, she forced herself to breathe slowly into the bag.

She'd researched her past problem of hyperventilating on Moose Ranch's internet and discovered the tingling around her mouth and in her fingers happened when she breathed too fast. She must have been doing that while worrying about everything and her anxiety had gotten ahold of her without her realizing it.

She'd learned that breathing too fast brought too much oxygen into her system. It could cause the carbon dioxide levels in her blood to fall, which caused blood vessels to narrow, which in turn decreased the blood flow to the brain making her feel lightheaded.

To rectify the problem, when it happened, she would have to breathe into a paper bag, inhaling the carbon dioxide she'd exhaled to level out the oxygen and correct the problem.

Within a few minutes, the tingling in her lips and fingers began to subside. Okay, she was going to be better now. But why couldn't she just keep it together? Why couldn't she just be normal like everyone else and not freak out over things?

Emotions overwhelmed her and tears welled in her eyes, blurring the view of the desolate blue lake surrounded with pine trees and rocky shoreline.

She had to stop catastrophizing. Her family was fine.

She inhaled a few more times and then removed the paper bag, being careful when she folded it, knowing she may need it again. Her hands trembled as she put the bag away under the cockpit seat. When she straightened, nausea rolled through her.

Oh, great. Morning sickness. Just what she needed on top of everything else.

Perspiration blossomed across her forehead as she searched for something to puke in. She found nothing. She headed for the door, slid it open and vomited into the lake.

Luke frowned as he gazed through the binoculars and watched a woman heaving into the lake from the bush plane that had landed moments ago.

For a split second, it pissed him off that someone dare puke into his drinking water, but then concern gripped him. Maybe she was in trouble? Maybe she was having a health issue? He didn't see any movement in any of the plane's windows.

Was she alone?

His frown deepened. He should turn his back on her. She was none of his concern.

But he just couldn't stop watching. It wasn't every day that someone flew to his secluded lake.

At first he'd thought a friend was flying in, but he hadn't recognized the plane. Then figured maybe someone was checking out the scenery or was having engine trouble. They had radios on those planes, she could call for help if she needed it.

But that would bring more people and he didn't want people around. He preferred his loneliness.

He kept watching her. She didn't move from the plane door. Yeah, maybe she was in trouble.

Luke sighed. He knew he was going to regret what he was about to do.

JJ didn't notice the puttering sound of an approaching motorboat until it was almost upon her. After puking her guts out, sucking in the fresh afternoon air and crying because she'd once again broken down with anxiety, she felt a bit better. But nausea continued to cling to her tummy and she didn't feel comfortable getting the plane up into the sky quite yet.

She just wanted to sit at the open door, enjoy the sunny breeze blowing against her sweaty forehead, dangle her legs over the edge of her plane and appreciate the scenery.

The shoreline was rocky and littered with gnarled driftwood and floating logs. This lake was beautiful and yet hauntingly quiet at the same time.

But where was that motorboat she was hearing?

She leaned a bit forward to slide a look along the side of the plane when a man about her age suddenly appeared. He sat at the back of a red aluminum boat. One arm was behind him holding a steering bar that protruded from the white motor, and his other hand was raised in a friendly wave.

Oh geez. She should get out of here. She was alone and she had no idea who he might be. He could be a deranged lunatic.

Her heart began to hammer with fear.

"Hello!" he called out as he cut the engine and let his boat drift slowly toward her.

"Hi, where did you come from?" she asked, praying she didn't start to hyperventilate again because she was once again breathing way too fast.

"My cabin is right over there. Up on the hill, behind those white pines on the peninsula."

He pointed south and she was surprised to see the outline of a small log cabin tucked behind some trees. She hadn't noticed it when she'd been studying her surroundings.

The man wore a tattered green fishing hat with lures of different sizes and colors all over it. He had unkempt shoulder length dark brown hair and brown eyes. His chin and cheeks were hidden behind a scruffy brown beard and moustache. He was dressed in a pair of blue jean shorts that had seen better days, a short-sleeved dark blue shirt and he wore running shoes.

She got more uneasy when she noticed what looked like burn scars on both his arms. Maybe he *was* he an escaped prisoner hiding out here?

*Oh, JJ! Stop! He's probably just a fisherman on vacation!*

"I thought I'd best check if you're okay?" he said in a quiet voice as the boat drew closer.

Heat from embarrassment fused her cheeks as she realized he might have actually seen her puking. Had he?

She noted the binoculars dangling from his neck.

Oh, dear. He had seen.

"I'm fine. Just pregnant."

His eyes widened in apparent surprise.

"Sorry, I didn't mean to just blurt it out. Just got the news yesterday. It was a huge surprise for us. I was up in the air when morning sickness hit, so I decided to land." She opted not to mention she'd been hyperventilating due to an anxiety attack.

He stared at her with a cute little grin on his face. And suddenly she felt at ease with him. She was usually a good judge of character, and he did seem harmless.

"You wouldn't by chance have some crackers back in your cabin, would you? I've got some bad nausea and crackers helped during my first pregnancy."

He brightened. Definitely not a killer.

"As a matter of fact, I do. Would you like a can of ginger ale too? My sister swore ginger ale helped settle her stomach during her pregnancies. She has three kids."

"Three kids. Wow. That's what I'm planning too. Yes, ginger ale would be great. Thank you."

He nodded.

"Okay, back soon."

He started his engine, and she grimaced at the whiff of gasoline as he angled the boat away from her plane and puttered toward his cabin.

Despite her nausea, JJ smiled and patted her little baby bump.

"You'll have a big sister, and maybe a baby brother or baby sister sometime in the future," she said out loud, hoping her unborn child could hear her.

"You'll be right in the middle. A big sister who will look out for you and a little sister or brother that you can boss around. That would be so cool, wouldn't it?"

She laughed when she felt the tiniest of a kick. Maybe newbie had heard her? Wouldn't that be something.

Once inside his cabin, Luke quickly grabbed the package of crackers from the cupboard. Then he hesitated as he eyed his pie crust recipe written on paper sitting on his kitchen counter. Maybe he could give it to her, so she wouldn't be frightened of him. He shoved it into his jeans back pocket and then headed down to the lake where he pulled on a rope attached to the end of his dock. A net filled with cans and bottles appeared out of the water. From the net he withdrew a couple of cans of ginger ale and then gazed at the few bottles of beer in there.

He frowned and shook his head.

No. No more beer. No more feeling sorry for himself and drowning his sorrows in booze. If he'd been drunk today; he wouldn't have been able to help that pilot.

He gently dropped the net back into the dark depths of the lake.

The cans of ginger ale were nice and cold in his hands as he placed them onto the bottom of his motorboat along with the package of crackers and sat down.

Excitement rushed through him as he pulled the cord on the motor and it roared back to life. He smiled as he angled the boat toward the big, white float plane that bobbed in the middle of the lake.

His earlier attitude of her not being his business had disappeared. He was glad he'd been here to help her. That's what he'd used to do in the past before his life had been destroyed. He'd helped save people and fought forest fires to help animals. It had always made him feel good.

Man, he hadn't felt this alive in one hell of a long time and he owed it all to that pregnant pilot lady.

• • ✺ • •

*GARY GUNTER'S FUNERAL Home, Toronto, Ontario*

Staring down at her dead husband's body, Jenna fought back the anger that had been raging inside of her since Tim's death. She'd just dropped off the clothes for his viewing that would be later tonight and had popped into this cold room where Tim was being housed.

She'd been allowed to come in and see him only because she knew the owner of the funeral home. Gary and Tim had been best friends through childhood and they'd remained in contact. Gary had agreed when she'd asked to see Tim privately.

"You bastard," she whispered to her husband's pale face.

Emotions, thick and raw, seared through her.

After years of a tumultuous marriage, they had finally gotten into a good groove again. Had finally decided to start a family and she had stupidly hoped a baby would save their marriage.

"You son of a bitch. You have some bloody nerve dying on me."

She could just scream at him.

Instead, she bit back a sob as she gazed at his blue lips.

"Why did you have to die on me now? Huh? All those times I caught you screwing around on me, I wanted you dead. And now that we finally are...were getting it together again, you decide to fuck off on me, permanently."

There was a knock at the door and Jenna straightened.

Gary cracked open the door and stuck his head inside.

"We need to get him ready."

She nodded and stood. The next time she saw her husband would be during the viewing. She'd said privately what she'd come to say. She felt just a little bit better.

Gary was waiting for her at the door.

"Thanks, Gary. I appreciate it," she said.

He nodded and she brushed past him.

A moment later she was outside in the fresh air and the warm sunshine. Instinctively her hand settled over her belly.

She needed to be strong now. For the baby.

• • ✤ • •

*PEARSON AIRPORT – TORONTO, Ontario*
   *4 p.m.*

"There she is!" Mitch gave out an excited shout from beside Brady and pointed to the petite sandy-blonde haired woman who was madly waving at them.

At first he didn't even recognize his youngest sister, Ginny. She looked thinner than he remembered and she'd dropped the tomboy look. No more jeans and frumpy hoodies that she loved to wear. No more bangs and waist long hair.

Instead, her hair was parted in the middle and had been cut to midback length. And she wore it in a lone braid. He swore this was the first time he'd seen her wearing a dress since she'd been little. His mother hadn't been able to get her into one from the moment she'd been able to talk. This dress was black and elegant and he wondered what had brought about such a transformation.

The grim desolation gripping Brady since Jenna's heart-breaking phone call early this morning, suddenly left him.

"Looks like runt may have herself a man," Mitch chided as they hurried to meet Ginny.

Runt, their nickname for her. They'd always kidded her about being the runt of the litter.

"Don't embarrass her with your stupid comments, Mitch. She looks good," Brady chided.

"Yeah, well, she's still the runt of the family. Man, I have missed bugging her," Mitch laughed. Brady could see the mischief twinkling in Mitch's blue eyes.

He couldn't take his eyes off his baby sister who just kept smiling and waving at them from the other side of the glass partition. She was quite happy to see them.

As they drew closer, Brady noticed her cheeks seemed a bit gaunt. But seeing her smiling face, which reminded him of his mother at that age from the pictures he'd seen in the family photo albums, had him forcing himself to bite back a thick well of emotion that suddenly got stuck in his throat.

Man, he'd missed Ginny.

Mitch got to her first. His brother dropped his small suitcase, let out a whoop of tremendous joy, that had nearby people smiling, and he lifted her feet full off the ground as he hugged her.

"Hey, runt! You are looking hot! What poor man have you reeled in?"

"Shut up, duffus!" Ginny giggled and pounded Mitch on his chest. He laughed and put her down.

When she saw Brady, she burst into tears and ran into his outstretched arms.

"Just ignore Mitch. He's being a butt-head, as usual," Brady soothed.

He sensed she wasn't upset about anything Mitch had said, but just glad to see them.

Having her wrap her arms around his neck as he picked her up with her wildly kissing his cheeks reminded him how precious life was. How they'd almost lost her years ago on that horrible snowy night when their parents had died.

"How are you doing?" he asked her as she let go of him and dropped her back to her feet.

"Doing good," Ginny replied as she wiped away her tears with the back of her hand and she was smiling again.

"Heard you guys hooked up with significant others. You both look well-fed and content. And Brady congratulations on your daughter! I've been meaning to drop in, but work has been terrible and I just haven't been able to get away. I will come soon to see my niece. Thank you so much for sending so many pictures. She is absolutely adorable."

"How is Jenna?" Mitch asked.

"She's putting up a good front. Come on, I've booked rooms for you."

Brady and Mitch grabbed their suitcases and followed Ginny.

# Chapter Five

"JJ should have been back by now, or at the very least called to let us know what's happening. She's been gone for too many hours," Dan commented as he stood in the front yard of the ranch house with Rafe, who held Chrissy.

Even Chrissy was gazing down the slope toward the shimmering blue lake, waiting for her mamma to come home.

It was four in the afternoon. The sun was still high enough in the sky, hardly any wind for JJ to deal with and no clouds to screw with her visual.

Yet there was no float plane docked at the dock.

"I'm sure she has a good reason," Rafe replied. He was trying to sound casual but Dan could hear the undertone of concern in Rafe's voice. That just made him even more nervous.

Rafe continued talking.

"Maybe Brady and Mitch couldn't get a charter flight so maybe she's waiting with them, right little Christmas?" Rafe said in a baby voice as he focused his attention to Chrissy who was now blowing bubbles with her spit.

Dan's heart clenched with love at the sight of the little girl curled up in Rafe's embrace. Man, she was so cute. Rafe had dressed her up today. In a sailor outfit. She looked adorable wearing a white pleated skirt over her bulky diapers and a sleeveless navy-blue top with bright red bowknot dangling from her chest.

Ordinarily he would steal her away from Rafe and kiss her chubby little cheeks and talk baby talk with her too, but today was anything but normal. There had been a death in the family.

"She would have radioed in and let us know. Something is wrong," Dan insisted. Something in his gut was just nagging at him that she should have been back by now.

"Geez, don't say shit like that in front of the baby," Rafe hissed. His dark brows burrowed into a disapproving frown.

"Don't swear in front of the kid," Dan snapped back. Irritation made him curse softly.

"Look who's talking," Rafe muttered and started chatting in baby talk tone to Chrissy again. Dan just didn't have the patience to hang around and listen. He needed to do something. Anything to find out what was wrong.

"I'm going to hail her on the radio and see if she's okay," he said.

Usually they didn't call when she was flying because they didn't want to distract her, but this time he'd make an exception.

Without waiting for a reply from Rafe, he headed back inside.

Man, things were heading south pretty fast today. Tim dead. Brady gone and now JJ was missing. He should have known something else was going to happen today. Shit always happened in threes.

He just hoped she had a good explanation for why she hadn't contacted them. She had a radio in her plane. If she needed help, she would call someone.

Dan swallowed and grimaced. Unless something catastrophic had happened and she wasn't able to call for help?

Dread crawled up Dan's spine. If something happened to her he swore he would lose his mind. She was carrying another baby. She shouldn't even be flying and putting herself and the newbie at risk. Man, what if her plane had gone down again?

*Oh man! Stop the bullshit! Call her!*

He cursed and headed into the office and stopped when he thought he might be hearing the low drone of an airplane. He raced to the window and opened it. There was only the whisper of the wind as it gently rustled the branches of the pine trees at the treeline. A brown rabbit hopped across the side yard and a woodpecker cracked its beak against a tree somewhere in the distance.

Had he imagined the sound of the plane?

*Dammit, JJ! Where are you?*

He was about to turn away from the window when he heard the noise again. The purr of a plane. Not too far off.

Excitement and worry collided.

It could be a plane just be passing by. Or someone else might be flying in to give them bad news about JJ?

Dan stood still and waited. His heart pounded in his ears. He could hear the engine clearly now.

It could be JJ. It sounded like her plane. From this angle at this window he couldn't see most of the lake so if she was back, she would be flying in from the south and then heading toward the east end of the lake before turning and then splashing down, like she always did.

Was it her?

Every part of his body jumped when Rafe let out a shout. He didn't know what Rafe had said, but before Dan knew it, he was rushing down the hallway, into the mud room and then outside.

Rafe was already halfway down to the dock, pointing to the lake. Chrissy was clenching her fists and waving her chubby arms. She always did that when she was really excited.

Relief poured through him as he spied the white plane flying in from the east. She'd already turned and was descending. The white pontoons of the bush plane hit the blue water with a gentle white splash as she touched down. Then she was angling toward their dock, the roar of the engines getting louder as she came closer.

Rafe was covering Chrissy's ears and laughing.

Dan smiled. She was back.

Thank you, Lord! She was home!

. . ⚓ . .

"WHERE HAVE YOU BEEN? We've been worried sick!" came Dan's angry shout as he hunched over and began to secure the plane to the dock with the thick ropes she'd tossed out the doorway only moments ago.

Irritation welled up inside of her.

"With a welcome like that, I should have stayed away longer," she snapped and immediately regretted her sharp answer.

Thankfully, Dan didn't say anything as he continued to tie down the plane. But she could tell he was upset in the way muscles flexed in his jaw. Thankfully, Rafe had taken Chrissy further down the dock when JJ had angled the plane closer. She liked that he'd been cupping her ears, helping to protect them from the loud noise of the engines.

Just seeing her little girl snuggled in Rafe's strong arms, her pudgy arms waving around and her little legs jerking with excitement made swells of emotions burst through her. Despite Dan's brisk welcome, she was glad to be home.

She laughed when Chrissy kicked Rafe in his upper belly and he let out an exaggerated oomph.

Her baby had missed her and the guys had been worried too. She'd realized it with Dan's retort and now with Rafe's overly large, forced smile and her wiggling daughter.

She was still feeling shaky and tired from her panic attack. Thankfully, Lucas had come to her rescue with crackers and cold cans of ginger ale in that puttering aluminum boat. The combination of food and drinks had somewhat settled her tummy. His easy-going attitude had put her at ease too.

She'd sat in the doorway of the plane; he'd sat in his boat and they'd conversed in the middle of the lake. He'd even given her a hand-written recipe for a scrumptious pie that would "knock her socks off," making her promise that if she were ever in the neighborhood again, to drop in with a homemade pie.

She'd promised she would. They hadn't shared very personal questions but when she'd told him she was from Moose Ranch, he'd asked if it was close to Snowy Creek Ranch. She'd said yes and he'd smiled asking if she knew Daegen, one of the owners there. She'd said she did and he'd become quite cheerful telling her that they were friends and Daegen came to visit sometimes. Slowly he'd opened up to her and admitted he lived in that cabin all year around, which made her wonder why. But she hadn't wanted to pry, so she hadn't asked.

Right now though, she didn't want to think about Lucas anymore. All she wanted to do was hug her baby. She walked along the dock toward Rafe and her wild child.

"Oh, you look so adorable in that outfit!" JJ called out.

"She picked it out herself!" Rafe called back.

"She has good taste," JJ complimented. But she knew Rafe was the one who'd dressed her, as this was his favorite outfit on her.

As JJ drew closer, she held out her arms to her daughter, and Chrissy began to cry. Within a second, she had her warm, wiggly sweetheart wrapped in her arms.

"I missed you too, chubby girl," JJ said as she kissed her daughter's pudgy wet cheeks and inhaled her fresh baby powder scent. She swayed her gently and hummed softly until Chrissy settled down.

"Glad you're home safe. She's overdue for her nap," Rafe said softly as they started up the trail.

Suddenly she just didn't want to talk to the guys, but she knew they wouldn't let her get away so easy.

And she was right

"So? What happened?" Dan asked as he joined them.

"Morning sickness. I landed the plane in a lake and waited it out." She had rehearsed her excuse, not wanting to mention her panic attack and hyperventilating.

"Told you something had happened," Dan growled to Rafe.

"Shush." She heard Rafe's reply.

"You don't look so good," Rafe commented as they crossed the front yard.

"That's because the sickness is still here," she admitted.

She should tell them the whole truth. Tell them that in her panic she had put herself and her unborn child into danger by landing her plane in a lake she'd never been to before. The pontoons could have hit a submerged log or rock or she could have miscalculated the distance of the lake and slammed into the shore.

She'd broken a rule in not radioing traffic control informing them she was diverting from her flight plan. Another plane could have been in the airspace she'd ventured into and they could have crashed midair. Sure there wasn't much traffic in these parts, but nonetheless she had made a serious aviation mistake.

"Sorry, I should have called. But a nice gentleman came to my rescue in his boat with crackers and ginger ale. We chatted and we lost track of time."

She was thankful when they didn't badger her any more on the subject, but she knew they'd be curious about this man. Questions would be coming once she felt better.

As she ascended the stairs and entered the mud room, Chrissy nestled heavily against JJ's chest and began rubbing her eyes.

"Time for a nap, hey, baby girl?" JJ whispered as she watched her daughter's eyelids flutter sleepily.

"I can put her down. You should try to have some food. Even a little. Maybe it will help settle your stomach. I made up a nice batch of macaroni and cheese and baked some steaks. Nothing heavy," Rafe said.

Ordinarily she would devour Rafe's delicious steaks but the queasiness rippled through her tummy at the smell of the spices permeating the air.

"Maybe later. I'm just going to lie down and take a nap with Chrissy."

"You rest. When you get up, we'll make you some chamomile tea," Rafe said as he headed into the kitchen.

JJ nodded.

She strolled towards the stairs and frowned when Dan followed her. He knew better than to lift Chrissy out of her arms and carry her up himself. Past experience proved any movement out of her arms into another set of arms when she was sleepy, would upset her.

"Are you really alright?" Dan asked softly as she began to ascend the stairs. Thankfully, he didn't follow her up.

"I'm fine," she answered. At least she hoped she would be.

"Okay, sleep tight," he replied.

JJ nodded. She was too tired to strike up a conversation. The bed wouldn't get to her soon enough.

. . ⚓ . .

AFTER A SHORT NAP, JJ was famished and she felt so much better. All the dreadful thoughts about Tim's death and her panic-stricken plane ride had vanished.

She felt normal again.

She'd gone down to the kitchen and discovered Rafe and Dan feeding Chrissy. There had been more food plastered on the two guys than in Chrissy's plate and JJ hadn't had such a good laugh in quite some time.

They'd insisted she sit and Dan had served her supper of macaroni and cheese, a big juicy baked steak and vegetables drizzled with butter. She'd had no problem devouring her food and the guys joked that it looked like she was eating for more then two.

After supper, she'd carried Chrissy down to the dock where they'd watched another brilliant sunset. Pink-tinged cauliflower shaped white clouds had reflected upon the choppy waves, giving a breathtaking view. A beaver swam with a large branch in its mouth, heading toward the west end of the lake where it had a house made of branches, sticks and mud.

As twilight came, the surrounding forest descended into darkness and the air quickly turned cool. She'd brought her daughter back inside where the three adults had entertained her by playing hide and seek and peekaboo. One of them would cover Chrissy's eyes, while the other two would hide. Then they'd laugh as her eyes widened in surprise and then Chrissy would smile or giggle when one of them were found in a closet or behind a sofa.

Brady called too and she'd loved hearing his voice. He sounded so much better than he had this morning. He'd said Jenna was holding her own and they would be going to Tim's viewing tonight and the funeral was already tomorrow. After that, he'd discuss with Jenna her plans. When JJ said goodbye to him, she'd handed the phone to Rafe and Dan who were excited to talk with him. It really was sweet to see the two men laughing and joking with him as if Brady were a long-lost friend they hadn't seen in years instead of having seen him just this morning.

While they'd conversed via speakerphone about the ranch, she'd given Chrissy a bath and noticed her fists were scrubbing her eyes. She was tired, the poor little thing. They'd wiped her out with dinner, their outing into the fresh air and playing with her.

JJ had decided to put her down for the night and then Dan had offered to back out of their night together, but she'd insisted she felt much better. She was craving to have his arms around her and wanted him in her bed tonight.

She'd just finished blow drying her hair when heard a soft knock at her bedroom door.

JJ smiled. Dan was such a gentleman.

She called him in and left her bathroom to find him in the bedroom, dressed in his pyjamas. He must have just finished his shower as well because his hair was damp and he smelled softly of soap. He grinned when he saw her and her heart clenched with love for him.

"Our man slave, Rafe, is downstairs cleaning up. So, where would you like to spend the night? Your place or mine?" he said and wiggled his eyebrows.

His teasing remark made her laugh and then she dropped her towel, which was the only thing she wore. His green eyes widened with surprise and appreciation as he gazed upon her. Then he held out his hand and she took it.

He pulled aside the comforters and sheet on her bed allowing her to climb in. She crawled into bed and moved over closer to the wall and watched as he removed his pajama top and then his bottoms.

Her pussy clenched with excitement and she blew out a tense breath as his cock arrowed out and upward like a mighty uncoiling serpent. Then he slipped into bed beside her and covered them with the snug sheet and comforters.

They both turned onto their sides, facing each other and he reached out and caressed his thumb upon her chin.

"You're so beautiful, JJ. I can't get enough of just looking at you, sweetie."

"Compliments like that will get you everything your heart desires," she teased.

Dan chuckled and then his gaze soon grew serious.

"About today, I'm sorry for being so short with you. It's just that when you came home late—"

She didn't want to go into his worries for her safety, so she lifted her hand and touched her fingers to his lips. She shook her head, indicating he be quiet. He shut up but continued caressing her chin. She watched his face as she skimmed her fingertips over his slightly parted lips, up across his right cheekbone and then along his dark eyebrow and back down the slope of his nose, giving the tip of it a gentle tap before dropping her hand away.

She loved looking at his face. Loved every contour, every mole, every little blemish, and even the tiny cut on his chin that he must have made while shaving. Tonight, his face was bristle free and smooth as a baby's bottom.

She reached beneath the sheets, found and then wrapped her hands around his solid shaft. His Adams apple bobbed as he swallowed.

"Okay, you've got my attention, woman," he finally breathed.

"Good, now kiss me," she demanded.

"I can do that," he replied. His green eyes glittered with approval as she began massaging the length of his swollen shaft.

His gaze darkened as he held her chin with his hand and then slowly moved his head toward hers. She closed her eyes, moaning as his hot mouth claimed hers. It wasn't a sweet, gentlemanly kiss, but one of power and possession, which made desire explode throughout her. Her mouth opened to him and his tongue thrust inside like a warrior.

Hunger, deep and aggressive burned through her and she moved closer to him. She inhaled deeply, smelling the hint of soap and his unique spicy masculine scent. She brushed her nipples against his downy haired chest, loving the friction of his flesh against her buds.

His kisses became restless and urgent, sending sizzling waves of awareness through her. Pleasure was coming, she could feel the tremors. The need building.

She kissed him harder, heard his groans. His swollen cock jerked and trembled against her fingers, his rigid flesh engorging even more, his penis becoming hotter.

Without breaking the kiss, Dan was moving, coming over her and then she was able to bring his cockhead against her sensitive clitoris. Then he moved his hips back and forth and around and around and she used his cockhead as a stimulator, quickly bringing forth the arousing sensations she craved.

Soon she was tensing. Her pussy was swelling, her vagina clenching with want. Wetness poured down her channel, readying her for his impalement. Her breaths grew faster and faster right along with his.

"Now," she hissed against his mouth.

Without hesitation, he plunged his shaft into the cradle of her thighs, into her wet vagina. The pressure of his swollen erection buried deep within was intense and she loved how his throbbing flesh claimed her, jerking and growing inside of her.

They were belly to belly. Chest to chest. Mouth to mouth.

His kisses, hot and intense.

Then he withdrew.

She held onto his waist and he started thrusting into her.

He tore his mouth from hers and kissed her cheeks, her chin, her neck. She could feel his body tensing and the flaming need for release bursting through her.

"Harder, faster," she hissed. Letting him know she needed more.

He did her bidding, and she gasped as the fever heat she'd been craving spiralled and then exploded over her in shimmering, gut wrenching waves. She shivered, shook, and moaned, enjoying the pleasure flooding her. Her thighs trembled and her pussy convulsed, gripping Dan's shaft every time he entered, every time he withdrew.

Oh yes! This pleasure was what she needed. This was *exactly* what she needed, tonight.

Dan enjoyed her moans and the intoxicating clenching of her vagina wrapped around his throbbing cock. He loved the way her body tightened as she slipped into her orgasm. He wished he could bring her this pleasure forever.

She wanted it more than ever. He could feel it in his soul. Maybe the baby hormones had something to do with it, he didn't know, but all too soon his body shuddered as he entered his own climax.

Blades of pleasure spasmed up the length of his shaft and exploded into his scrotum and beyond. He went wild, his self control completely disintegrating. He thrust and pistoned into her wet heat like a madman.

And all too soon he was spurting into her. His sperm shooting deep inside as he joined her in the pleasure world they'd created.

Rafe stood outside JJ's bedroom door and listened to JJ's moans and Dan's groans. He blew out a tense breath and reached down and rubbed the aching bulge tenting his pants. He'd have to get his satisfaction in the shower tonight. But tomorrow night it was his turn with JJ and he'd give her some hot pleasure too.

His thoughts briefly turned toward Brady and Mitch. He hoped the brothers' company would bring some comfort to Jenna. He shook his head and pushed away the thoughts about the death of her husband.

Shit happened so fast. If he honestly thought about it, he would drive himself crazy at how fast things changed. But that was life. Ever changing.

Rafe blew out his breath as JJ's soft cries rippled through the air. His cock jerked painfully. He needed to concentrate on that shower.

Now.

• • ❧ • •

"WELL, THANK GOD, THAT'S over," Jenna complained as Brady, Mitch and Ginny flanked her on the way out of the funeral home.

Jenna frowned when no one answered her.

"Come on guys, don't be so gloomy. I need cheering up. Let's go to a bar, get drunk. Forget all this shit."

She wanted to drown her sorrows about Tim. Just completely forget he even existed and wasn't lying there in that godawful coffin. But then she remembered she shouldn't be drinking, due to the baby.

"Forget the bar," Mitch said. "Why don't we go back to the hotel, pig out on junk food and watch horror movies like we did when we were kids?"

Warmth flooded Jenna as the others chimed in agreement. Yeah, this is what she needed.

Family. Support and a major distraction. They all loved horror movies. This would be good to keep her mind off Tim.

*That bastard.*

Too bad her other siblings hadn't been able to make it. Well, her one remaining sister couldn't for sure, and she understood that reason as she was in prison. But the others were all scattered to the wind and Ginny hadn't been able to reach them.

Suddenly Ginny slipped her palm against Jenna's and took her hand just like when she'd been a kid. She squeezed Jenna's hand.

"It's all going to be okay," Ginny whispered and gave Jenna a wobbly smile. Tears bright in her blue eyes.

Ginny, the youngest and the most emotional of the siblings.

A torrent of grief shot through Jenna.

Her husband was dead. Just like that. How could anything ever be okay again?

She nodded. She needed to stay strong. For the baby.

Yeah, right.

Easier said, then done.

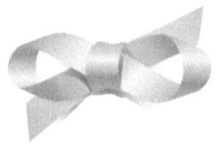

# Chapter Six

JJ awoke, still feeling pretty good. To her surprise, Dan had already left her bed.

Usually he hung around and they snuggled. But not this time. Then she remembered why. Moose Ranch was down one man and the guys would have to work harder until Brady returned. Anxiety suddenly clutched at the pit of her stomach as to the reason Brady had left.

JJ shook away the dread, whipped aside her covers, and quickly got out of bed, knowing that if she stayed here, her thoughts about Jenna's husband's sudden death may soon put her into anxiety attack mode.

She needed to distract herself.

She donned her robe and crossed the hall to Chrissy's room. The crib was empty. Not surprising. One of the guys had already taken her downstairs.

A sudden attack of guilt pummelled her. They already had so much to do and she didn't want to put any more burden on them, so she decided to forgo a shower, quickly dressed and then headed downstairs, where she found Rafe feeding the baby.

He had dressed Chrissy in a yellow peasant top, bloomers, socks and a bright yellow bib. And her daughter's chubby cheeks were plastered with matching yellow squash. When Chrissy spied JJ, she smiled and if JJ didn't know any better, she could swear there was a glint of mischievous in Chrissy's twinkling blue eyes.

"Good morning, sunshine," Rafe called out when he noticed JJ watching them. He pointed to the skillet on the counter.

"Chrissy has already been cleaned and changed, so have a sit down. Breakfast is warming in the skillet. Take advantage of the down time while I finish feeding the kid."

*The kid.* Rafe's nickname for Chrissy.

JJ hurried over to her daughter and her heart burst with love as she bent over and hugged her baby, who cooed happily as JJ kissed her squash riddled warm cheeks.

"Good morning, what evil deeds are we up to here?" she asked as she straightened and licked some pureed squash off her own bottom lip.

"Hmm, doesn't taste that bad, does it, sweetheart?" JJ asked her daughter as Chrissy kicked out her feet with glee and then focused her attention to spitting out the spoonful of squash Rafe had just managed to get into her mouth.

"It's not as bad as it looks. I promise," Rafe said as he gazed up at JJ. Her breath locked in her lungs at his unmasked heated look.

Oh mercy, she could tell in the sultry way he looked at her that he wanted sex and truth be told, so did she, especially when she thought about last night with Dan. She focused her attention on other things about Rafe. He was dressed in a muscle illuminating black T-shirt, jeans and the drools of yellow squash splattered on his face.

"This seems to be a repeat performance of last night," JJ replied and couldn't help but laugh as she reached out and wiped some squash from Rafe's chin and another off his left cheek.

"Well, isn't mommy being rude?" he asked Chrissy in baby talk. Chrissy just stared back at him with wide eyes. But JJ could tell in the way the tips of Rafe's lips turned slightly upward that he was trying to keep himself from laughing.

"Go head, grab some grub. Coffee is fresh. Dan's already left. He'll be checking the Misty Lake quarter today and depending on if there is wolf trouble again, he might not come back tonight, but he'll check in around noon. He's outlined everything we're doing today and where we'll be. He put it up on the bulletin board in the office."

The bulletin board.

It was something they'd decided to do. Pinning notes to the board instead of having them lying around and possibly getting lost. Besides their co-ordinates, it always included their estimated time of arrival back home. ETA so they would know who was where in case someone didn't come home.

JJ nodded and poured herself a coffee trying hard not to let thoughts about something possibly going wrong with one of them while Brady was away. Thankfully, there were no signs of queasiness as the salty aroma of warming bacon and scrambled eggs drifted in the air.

*Yet.*

But the day is young, she reassured herself. She'd learned while carrying Chrissy that morning sickness did not just appear in the morning.

She watched as Rafe pressed another spoonful of squash against Chrissy's lips. She refused to open her mouth.

JJ frowned as a bit of anxiety rippled through her. Usually she waited for Brady to help coax food into their daughter. But with Brady gone, what was she going to do if Chrissy didn't eat? Her breast milk had mysteriously stopped at four months and JJ had been frantic. But her doctor had reassured her at the time that nothing was wrong after running some tests. It was why they'd gotten Chrissy on a formula and started introducing her to pureed food.

She shook those anxious thoughts away. If Chrissy refused to eat, she would drink the formula. All would be well. There was no need to needlessly worry about that. Her thoughts turned to why her breast milk had dried up in the first place. Maybe it was because she'd already been pregnant again and the doctor had never checked? Could be. Maybe there was nothing wrong with her as a mother, after all.

"What's on your agenda today?" she asked and drank some of the hot coffee to wash down the bacon and eggs. The coffee was nice and strong, just the way she liked it first thing in the morning.

"Checking on some pregnant cattle out in the northwest area. After that I'll continue planting up that way. Tractor is there from when I started a couple of days ago. I packed lunches for myself and Dan. And I put yours in the fridge." he said and tossed her a crooked grin that made her heart leap with excitement.

Gosh, he was so handsome. Chestnut brown hair that curled at the nape of his tanned neck, a slightly off-centre nose and those endearing brown eyes that reminded her of diving into chocolate pudding.

"My cooking is never as good as yours. But I figure you'll have your hands full with the little rascal," he said with a chuckle.

He returned his attention to Chrissy who smiled back at him. As he continued trying to coax food into her, JJ took the opportunity to chow down the bacon and eggs and drink the rest of her coffee.

"Am I right, chubby cheeks? You're going to be good for your mom today, aren't you?"

He nodded and opened his mouth encouraging her to eat. But she merely pressed her lips tighter together.

Rafe frowned.

"Well, looks like she's full. At least she ate her pablum and formula. That should get her some energy."

"That's fantastic. That will keep her for awhile," JJ replied, feeling satisfied now that there wouldn't be any catastrophe of her baby not eating.

She slid her empty plate into the kitchen sink and then headed to the coffee pot for another cup of steaming coffee.

"Want a refill?" she asked him.

"Nope, gonna head out."

He placed the spoon of squash into the almost full little bowl and JJ didn't have the heart to tell him that squash was better attempted on an empty belly at lunch or dinner, not after a good breakfast of pablum and formula.

She poured her second cup of coffee and caught the squeak of Rafe's chair as he stood.

A moment later, her breath caught as he came up behind her. He pressed his hard, muscular body against her back and his warm breath caressed her cheek as he gently nibbled on her earlobe. The unmistakable bulge of his erection pressing against her behind, had her breathing harder and her pussy clenching as she imagined him sliding his cock into her.

His hands curled over her hips like hot brands and he whispered into her ear.

"I heard you two last night."

"You did?" she replied, suddenly feeling hot and bothered remembering how Dan had pistoned into her bringing her so much pleasure.

"Yeah, and the cold shower I took didn't work, so I'll be looking forward to tonight. Our night."

He said the last two words so tenderly that she was about to turn around and shower him with "promises of a hot night coming" kisses, but he let her go and quickly grabbed his lunch pail off the counter.

Then he bent over and kissed Chrissy on her cheek.

"See you later, chubby cheeks. Take care of your mom. Have a great day, JJ!" he called out as he hurried down the hallway.

"You too! Bye!"

She hugged herself and giggled. She knew why he was in such a hurry to get out of here. That impressive bulge pushing up against her rear and his comment about tonight. Had he stayed any longer and she'd kissed him, she'd no doubt they would have put Chrissy in her playpen right along with the bowl of squash while the two of them ended up in bed together for a delicious quickie, delaying everything that needed to get done around the ranch. It wouldn't be the first time either.

The slam of the mud room door was followed by the clump of boots down the stairs and then it was quiet.

Chrissy was already busy sticking her fingers into the bowl of squash, so JJ strolled over to the slightly opened window and enjoyed her coffee as she watched a blue jay flittering into the bird feeder. She noticed Dan or Rafe had already filled it with sunflower seeds.

It was the same window that the bear had been gazing in. Had that only been a couple of days ago? Thankfully, remembering the bears didn't so much as make her flinch today.

She settled her free hand over her slightly rounded belly as a warm feeling enveloped her. It wasn't even forty-eight hours since she had the confirmation she was once again pregnant and she already loved her newbie with all her heart.

Oh dear, how was she going to handle having two little ones to look after when she had a ranch house to clean and three men to feed?

She shook her head and sipped on her hot coffee. The thought of complaining should not even be entering her mind. She had spent so many years in prison, never dreaming she would be so lucky to have three men who loved her unconditionally and having one baby with another one on the way.

JJ smiled at her daughter who was still occupied with the squash, her entire hands now covered with it as was the tray and her bib. The mess was going to fun to clean up, but her daughter was enjoying herself and that's all that truly mattered.

"Well, baby girl. Looks like it's just us two today."

Chrissy ignored her and JJ couldn't help but giggle.

No, she could not complain. How could she? She was the luckiest woman in the world.

. . ❧ . .

RAFE GRINNED WHEN HE finished checking the last pregnant cow. He was pleased. They all seemed to be doing well and he didn't anticipate any problems with this bunch. He figured they could give birth on their own without issues. It was a good thing they'd sold off the problem cows to slaughter last year, so Moose Ranch wouldn't have to move any to the barn in order to keep an eye on them, which was a good thing as it freed up time to get other work done.

Man, it sure had gotten hot today. The sun was beating down on him and it was still early in the morning. The weather forecast promised a chance of rain or thundershower this afternoon, so he'd best get to planting that seed in order for the rain to do its job.

He lifted his cowboy hat off his head and using his bandana he wiped perspiration off his forehead, plopped his hat back on and hopped onto the all-terrain vehicle.

In a second, the machine was purring and he angled the atv with attached trailer toward the gate in the distance. Due to a relatively dry spring, they'd been able to till and seed earlier than usual so they already had many meadows sowed with grass, legumes and other herbaceous plants for the cattle. Having extra homegrown feed was always better than running out. Last winter, they'd had to order more feed for the winter months and send JJ with the plane to pick it up. So they'd decided on cultivating additional meadows this year.

He was feeling pretty happy today despite what had happened yesterday with the news about Tim. He would have been happier too had he stayed home and made love to JJ, but there was much work to be done here today. He'd have to wait and enjoy her company tonight. There was nothing better than putting in a full day work, coming home to a well-cooked meal and a gorgeous sexy woman who enjoyed being shared by three men.

He hummed to himself as he drove along the edge of the meadow beneath the cool shade of the trees and passed the pregnant cows who grazed nearby. He stopped when he came to the gate. Moments later, he was on the other side motoring along the small trail they'd cut through the forest years ago when they'd first come here.

The three of them had worked like dogs from sunup to sundown and sometimes even by lamplight cutting out their wilderness homestead. The challenging work had paid off. There was plenty of money in the bank from their organic Angus beef sales, they knew what they were doing with the ranch and now they had JJ and Chrissy.

Man, he was so lucky having JJ. His heart clenched with love as he thought about his beautiful woman. Vulnerable, yet tough. Sweet, yet strong. She kept the ranch clean and worked like a well-oiled machine caring for all of them. Now she wanted to have this newbie baby here on the ranch, like she'd done with Chrissy.

He frowned, his earlier happiness disintegrating. He had been a nervous wreck when she'd gone into labor and the midwife had been delayed because of severe weather. Thankfully, the birth had gone without incident but he'd have to make it a point to read up on things that could go wrong during a pregnancy. Just in case.

Of course, he could try to talk her into staying in Thunder Bay near a hospital. Then when the time came she was only a hop, skip and a jump away from the medical facility. Unfortunately in the determined look she'd given them the other day when she said she wanted the baby here with the same midwife, he was quite sure he wouldn't be able to persuade her to leave.

He pushed away his uneasiness and smiled as the towering pine trees suddenly slipped away and he cruised into the sunlit meadow he'd be seeding today. Everything he needed was already here. The land had been freshly tilled, the black rows were ready to be seeded. The bright blue tractor and equipment were right where he'd left them parked at the far end of the meadow. He had the seeds tucked under a large tarp in the attached trailer and he was ready to get to work.

He shut off the machine and gazed at his watch. Already nine. He'd need to get a move on if he intended to finish before nightfall. He removed his lunch bag from the trailer and in minutes he had his food hanging off a nearby branch. It was high enough up and out so the bears couldn't get to it, if they came around and smelled it.

Usually he kept his food in a bear proof cooler, but he'd opted to just grab his lunch pail and run before caving into his desires to take JJ into the bedroom and make mad passionate love to her. His cock felt thick and heavy as he thought about her. He loved the way her eyes scrunched up tight when she climaxed. He enjoyed watching too when Dan and Brady made love to her. However, tonight he would have her all to himself.

He smiled, grabbed his gloves and started hauling out a heavy bag of seed from the trailer.

Yup, he was one fortunate guy.

. . ~ . .

THE MORNING PROGRESSED slowly and JJ felt surprisingly calm as she kept herself distracted from any negative thoughts that dare enter her mind.

First, she'd given Chrissy a bath, changed her clothing, then she'd set her into the upstairs playpen for some tummy time with her stuffed animals while she'd changed the sheets, made the beds and did some sweeping. Afterwards they'd gone downstairs and as she'd whipped up a chocolate cake for tonight's dessert and cut up vegetables for soup, she talked to Chrissy about what she was making for supper. But Chrissy ignored her and watched the birds fluttering around the birdfeeder just outside the window.

Later, while the washing machines were doing their duty with the sheets, she went on a leisurely walk around the yard with her baby held snugly in her arms. She'd sing to her and teach her how to clap her hands. Then they went into the barn out of the morning heat. When the loons started their lonesome cries down on the lake, Chrissy's pudgy legs began kicking, indicating she wanted to go and watch those birds too.

So, JJ had carried her down to the lake where she was pleasantly surprised to find several black and white patterned loons with their grayish brown feathered babies floating near the dock upon the gentle waves. Three babies sat on one loon's back, while four others straggled behind, furiously paddling to keep up with their parents.

The serene sight made her smile and she sat in one of their four Adirondack chairs near the end of the dock and bounced her happy daughter on her knees as they watched the birds. The gentle breeze smelled of pine and the sunny blue skies were filled with giant white cottony clouds.

Every time an adult loon called out with a mournful cry, Chrissy giggled and kicked her legs. Her sparkling blue eyes stayed wide open with curiosity as she listened and stared. It was super amazing how her daughter could gaze at something for what seemed like hours without losing interest. But that was okay, it gave JJ a bit of a break from her work anyway.

To JJ's surprise, Chrissy was on her best behaviour today. When the loons decided to swim to other side of the lake, she had no trouble bringing her daughter back to the ranch house where she ate all her late morning snack of mashed peas and formula and now JJ had had no trouble changing her and putting her down for a nap in the crib in the nursery.

Her heart burst with love as she watched her little angel's eyes flutter sleepily while she sucked on her pacifier and scrunched up her fists close to her eyes. A moment later, she fell asleep.

Quietly, JJ cracked open the window to allow some fresh air into the warm room, when suddenly the rumble of a plane caught her attention. Just then the phone started to ring. She slipped out of the nursery and rushed to one of the bedrooms to answer the phone. When she picked it up, no one was on the other line. From the windows in this room she clearly saw the lake and a yellow floatplane splashing down.

Huh, it looked like she was having company. The only person she knew who had a bright yellow plane like that one, was her midwife and they didn't have any scheduled visits. She brightened as she realized this was perfect timing. She would ask Layla if she would be interested in delivering her second baby.

She headed downstairs to put on the coffee for her surprise guest. As she got the coffee percolating in the machine, she grabbed a couple of mugs, plates and cutlery and quickly set the table. She had just turned off the burner where a pot of vegetable soup had been simmering, when she heard a loud knock on the mud room door.

Before JJ could so much as call out to Layla to enter, her midwife had already opened the mudroom door and was shouting.

"Hello! Anyone home! I've got an emergency delivery in progress! I need help!"

Layla's shout was followed by a moan.

Oh dear!

"I'm here!" JJ yelled.

Adrenaline shot through her as she quickly rushed down the hallway. When Layla saw JJ, she looked relieved.

A tall woman leaned heavily against Layla, who struggled to keep the woman upright. Actually the woman looked more like a gangly teenager. She was alarmingly pale and her brown eyes were bright with pain. She wore black track pants and a pink maternity top that did nothing to hide the fact that she was extremely pregnant. JJ immediately suspected the teen was carrying more than one baby.

"Hi JJ! I am so glad you are here! Can we use a bedroom? I've already called the doctor. He's on his way here. I tried to call you, but I had to hang up because she had another contraction."

So that's who'd just phoned. JJ immediately rushed to the woman's other side, wrapped her arm around her big waist and helped her walk down the hall.

"There's a guest bedroom right down the hall. It's very close," JJ encouraged.

Goodness! The girl's stomach was so swollen that JJ wondered why she wasn't in the hospital.

"T...Thank you," the girl whispered. Her teeth were chattering as if she was freezing.

A couple of minutes later, they managed to get her seated on the edge of the bed and then Layla headed toward the bedroom door.

"JJ, please. Can you stay with her? I need to get my stuff out of the plane."

Layla didn't wait for an answer and was gone.

*Oh dear Lord, just hurry*! She did not like how this girl looked. She had never seen anyone so pale.

Except her mother, when JJ had found her dead on the floor.

# Chapter Seven

JJ pushed the horrible memory aside.

This girl and her babies were not going to die. Not on her watch. Not if she could help it. She quickly placed a comforter over the shoulders of the shivering girl.

"I...I guess I should have listened to...the doctor...and stayed near...hospital," she said between her chattering teeth.

"Hindsight is always twenty twenty. But don't you worry, Layla delivered my firstborn and she did a wonderful job. I'm going to ask her to deliver my second one too. I just found out I'm pregnant. Layla doesn't know yet," JJ said with a smile.

Her eyes widened with surprise and JJ caught the briefest glimpse of a grin. She was a pretty girl with short brown hair, a spatter of cute freckles on her cheeks and a sweet, upturned nose. There was an unusual amount of acne on her forehead and chin.

"How old are you?" JJ blurted.

"Eighteen."

"Oh, you're so young," another blurt. JJ had been around this age when they'd shipped her off to prison.

"I get...that a lot. Too...young for...twins."

So, she *was* having twins, just like she'd suspected.

"I'm JJ, what's your name?"

"Titania, Tita for short." The teenager scrunched her eyes closed and gasped with pain; her knuckles went whiter as she clenched her fists.

"I'm pleased to meet you. I wish it had been under different circumstances, but it is what it is. Where do you live?" she figured she may as well try to keep the girl distracted while they waited for Layla's return. But remembering her own night of pain waiting for Chrissy to be born, all she wanted was for people to shut up and take away her pain. But try as she might, she just couldn't keep quiet while this girl suffered.

"Thirty...miles north. We have a homestead...on...on a beautiful lake...off the grid."

"Where is your husband? He should be here with you for moral support." JJ cursed herself for asking that question. Perhaps she wasn't even married.

"Out east...oil worker."

"That's a good paying job. It will come in handy especially when you are having twins," JJ said. She knew she was being overly cheerful, but she couldn't help herself. Seeing this teenager in such distress seemed to bring out a nervous enthusiasm in her.

She stopped talking as the girl moaned, once again gripped in the throes of another contraction. She figured it had only been half a minute since the last one.

"Yes...he's...making us money," Tita whispered after the contraction ebbed.

"You were living all alone out there?" JJ asked.

Tita nodded. Huge tears bubbled in her eyes.

Dear Lord. This young woman was so brave to be alone while she was so hugely pregnant.

"I miss him," she whispered.

"I know," JJ consoled as she reached out and squeezed her hand.

"I had hoped...he would be with me...by now. I called...him...last night...when labor started. He said...he was coming."

JJ swallowed. Last night? She gazed at the clock. It was noon. The poor girl had to be exhausted being in labor for so long.

From somewhere outside came the drone of a plane.

For a few seconds, panic pounded JJ. Was Layla leaving them? Would JJ have to deliver the babies on her own? She reined in her unrealistic thoughts and resisted the urge to run to the window to make sure she wasn't being abandoned.

It wouldn't be the first time she'd helped deliver a baby. But that other time Rafe had been with her and he'd done most of the work, aside from the mother. It had also been an emergency birth.

"I hear another plane," the teenager gasped.

"It must be the doctor. Everything will be okay now," JJ reassured. She squeezed the girl's hand.

Oh God, she hoped it was the doctor.

"Please...make sure if something...h...happens to me. I want...my babies saved."

Alarm shifted through JJ.

"Nothing is going to happen to you or to your babies," she comforted. Although she wasn't so sure.

Where was Layla? What was taking her so long? What if Tita dropped a baby right out of her and it fell onto the floor?

JJ swallowed and blew out a tense breath. She needed to concentrate. Needed to focus and stop thinking bad stuff.

"Tell me, do you know their genders?" she asked.

Tita shook her head.

"You want it to be a surprise then, just like me."

The woman nodded, then bit her bottom lip as another convulsion ripped through her. Then she screamed.

Oh my goodness, how could someone endure such pain?

"Yes" Tita hissed a moment later.

"Okay, ladies. The doctor just landed. He should be up in a few minutes," Layla said as she burst into the bedroom. Her eyes were bright with excitement as she placed a very big duffel bag and a large, overstuffed black plastic bag upon the other side of the bed.

"JJ, if you would be so kind as to go out and greet him. I'll get Tita, ready."

JJ nodded, thankful to get away from the poor girl. She rushed from the room and stopped in the hallway for a moment to listen for Chrissy, but no sound came from upstairs. When she was satisfied her daughter was okay, she hurried outside and abruptly stopped.

On the path, hurrying towards her, were two men.

The one in front, was the shortest of the two. Perhaps six feet tall, clean-shaven, with an abundance of chestnut colored curly hair on his head and very wide shoulders. He wore black slacks and a light green long sleeved shirt. The sunlight glinted off what she perceived was a name tag on the left breast area of his shirt. He wore a large black knapsack and he carried a black doctor's bag. JJ figured he must be in his late twenties or early thirties.

When he saw her, he waved.

The second man appeared to be quite tall. Well over six feet. He was young. Maybe twenty. He was of thin build with shoulder length blonde hair and piercing green eyes that smiled, despite his worried look. He wore jeans and a dark green short sleeved T-shirt. He carried a duffel bag in each hand. Perhaps he was a very young doctor in training?

Above them the sun was shining with such a brightness, JJ wished for sunglasses or her floppy straw hat. Heat poured in shimmering waves into the yard where she stood and she spied blue jays and red cardinals cheerfully fluttering around the birdfeeder outside the kitchen window. The birds were totally oblivious of the turmoil unfolding around JJ.

A moment later, the two men joined her in the yard. She immediately noted the shorter of the men's name tag. Dr. William Brown.

"Hello! I'm Dr. Willie Brown. Thank you for letting us use your home. We really appreciate it," he said. He kept walking toward the house and JJ had to practically run to keep up with him. The other man followed with ease.

"No problem. Her contractions are less than half a minute apart," JJ said.

"Thank you. If you will show us the way please?" Dr. Brown said as he stopped at the bottom of the stairs, allowing her to pass.

JJ moved quickly up the stairs and they followed. She showed them into the mudroom and then down the hall where she stopped in front of the bedroom door, which was now closed.

She knocked gently.

"Come in. Please hurry," Layla called out.

JJ opened the door and the doctor rushed past her. She wasn't sure what to do, so she just stood in the doorway with the other man, who threw her a wobbly smile, but remained silent.

The pregnant woman was standing beside the bed, bent over at the waist, holding onto the night table for support. She now wore one of those blue hospital gowns that opened at the back. Layla stood over some medical instruments she had placed upon a pristine white cloth draped over the computer desk they had in the room. The comforters had been removed from the bed and pristine white sheets had been placed there.

The pregnant girl was breathing heavily. Perspiration glistened on her pale face. She looked quite terrified, but to JJ's astonishment, her look transformed from terror to one of immense relief when she spied the man standing beside JJ.

"Bobby. Thank God, you made it."

"Wouldn't miss this for the world, sweetheart. Can I come in?" His voice was deep and gravelly, surprising JJ by its strength.

The doctor waved him inside.

Bobby was at Tita's side, kissing her wet cheeks and looking at her so adoringly, JJ couldn't help but smile at the love that was so obvious between them.

Layla was speaking to the doctor in a low tone and the doctor's face looked grim and serious as he kept nodding.

JJ felt like an intruder standing in the doorway, yet she didn't want to interrupt or to leave, in case someone needed something.

Part of her wished Chrissy would cry out so she would have an excuse to leave and yet she wanted her daughter to sleep so she wouldn't be exposed to this trauma in the house. So she stood and waited and heard glimpses of the conversation between the doctor and the midwife. They were discussing a caesarean and also an emergency evacuation via helicopter.

The young couple seemed to be in their own little world, unaware of the conversation. Her husband was breathing and panting like Tita, encouraging her through the contractions. Then suddenly Layla and the doctor hurried over to JJ.

Dr. Brown held out a card to her.

"Can you give this number a call. Tell them I need an immediate evacuation, following a difficult birth of twins. Tell them I cannot get to the phone, but they need to hurry. Thanks," he abruptly moved back to the couple and began speaking to them.

Anxiety splashed through JJ as Layla began to talk to her.

"After that phone call, I'm going to need you to boil water," Layla instructed.

"How much water?" JJ asked, her thoughts twisting as she tried to remember the doctor's earlier instructions. She didn't want to forget anything.

To JJ's surprise, Layla grinned.

"For coffee. Lots of it."

JJ blinked.

"Okay," JJ nodded, feeling just a tinge of relief zip through her.

Layla smiled and winked.

"Thanks, hon. I'll just close the door, so they can have privacy."

JJ took her cue and headed for the kitchen.

Once there she grabbed the phone and quickly dialed the number on the card.

The phone rang once, twice and thankfully someone answered with the words, air ambulance. It was a woman.

JJ's heart was pounding at a rapid clip as she explained why she was calling. The woman on the other end asked JJ a bunch of medical questions that she couldn't answer, but she told the lady that the doctor had said he would not be able to come to the phone. But she had heard talk of a possible Caesarean. JJ gave them the coordinates to the ranch, and the woman asked if there were somewhere a helicopter could land and JJ explained yes, there was a long, cleared area just minutes northwest of the ranch. The woman gave JJ an ETA of two hours.

As JJ hung up, her hands were shaking and she blew out a tense breath.

Two hours. People could be dead in minutes out here without help.

*But that's the chance you take living here,* an inner voice pushed through her uneasiness. She reined in her restlessness and started up the coffee. She didn't hear any noises from the bedroom. No cries of pain. No encouraging words. Nothing.

Just dead silence.

Had the woman died? Had her babies died?

*Oh God, please let them be safe,* JJ fervently prayed as the stillness continued.

The ringing of the telephone made her jump and she quickly reached out and grabbed the receiver. Relief poured through her at Dan's voice.

"Hey, baby mama. Sorry I missed waking up next to you this morning. Hell, I already miss you like crazy. How's your day going?"

Oh, if you only knew, JJ silently said. She opted not to tell him what was happening. He'd most likely hurry right back and there wasn't anything he could do here now anyway.

"Going good here on my end. Chrissy is napping and I'm just grabbing a bite," she lied.

"Make sure you eat lots. You're eating for two, sweetheart," he replied. She could hear the humor in his voice.

"Lots of nutritious food. Like chocolate cake and oodles of coffee," she teased.

He groaned.

"Man, I wish I was there. Coffee, chocolate cake and you."

"Wish you were here too," she replied. And she truly meant it.

Having Dan, or Rafe here during this emergency, would have made her feel less jittery.

"How long are you going to be away?" she asked the dreaded question and tried hard to keep the desperation out of her voice.

"Well, there is lots of wolf activity. I've seen a pack of them. But no casualties as of yet where the beef are concerned. If there are any dead cattle, I haven't found them yet. Maybe our luck is turning and they'll leave Moose Ranch cattle alone. I plan on riding a few more hours to do surveillance before I turn in for the night over at Misty Lake. Then I plan on checking more pastures tomorrow morning."

JJ frowned. He wasn't coming home tonight, just like Rafe had mentioned might be the case.

"Are you going to miss me?" he asked cheerfully.

"Of course," she replied. Despite all that was happening around her, JJ smiled into the receiver. She sensed Dan was about to tease her.

"More than you miss the other guys? Wait don't answer that! I don't want you to get into any trouble with them."

JJ giggled.

"You know you're my one and only cowboy," she teased back.

"Good, that's what I wanted to hear. Okay, I will leave you to your cake and coffee, sweets. I should be back by mid afternoon tomorrow. Save me some of that cake."

"I will. Love you," she answered.

"Love you too, baby mama." his voice sounded thick and husky and she wished again he was here. Then the line went dead and JJ was thrust back into reality and the oppressing silence.

She stared at the coffee machine. The coffee steamed and the chocolate cake she had removed from the fridge earlier sat there on the counter untouched.

Suddenly queasiness rippled through her.

Oh damn! Morning sickness was kicking in. She sensed she wouldn't be able to get to the bathroom soon enough, so she scrambled for the kitchen sink, and promptly vomited.

. . ⚓ . .

RAFE SENSED SOMETHING was wrong, but he just didn't know for sure what. Awhile ago, he had heard a plane heading in the direction of the ranch house. And then, not too long after, he had heard another one.

Of course, it could have been the same plane circling around. But he didn't think so. It had sounded like two different engines.

Living out here in the northern wilderness, he had become attuned to the different noises in his surroundings. The clattering of woodpeckers, the cackle of wild turkeys. Sometimes, he heard the mews of beavers if he was near a swamp or lake, or growls of bears warning him to avoid their cubs.

He'd even become attuned to the sound engines, which were rare around here.

He'd turned off the tractor and retrieved his lunch when he'd heard the first plane, and then shortly after, the second plane.

There was no proof they'd landed in their lake, but uneasiness was whispering through him. He decided it was best to call JJ and check in on her. But when he had, the phone had gone directly to voicemail, which meant she had been on the line. He'd tried two more times.

Had there been an emergency?

Rafe shook away the adrenaline threatening to surge through him. He forced himself to finish his meal of bear steak sandwiches. He would call her again in a little while.

Surely, if there *had* been an emergency she would have called him.

Rafe nodded. He couldn't start panicking every time his imagination ran wild. If he did, he wouldn't get any work done. He nodded reassuringly to himself.

JJ was fine...but what if she wasn't?

· · ❧ · ·

"YOU ARE CORRECT. THE placenta has separated."

He gazed over at Layla and she read the concern in Willie's eyes. Ordinarily there was a small chance of a very bad outcome, but because they weren't in a hospital setting, things could become deadly here.

"What does that mean?" Tita's husband asked. His eyes darted back and forth like a deer caught in the headlights of a car.

"It means for the safety of mother and babies; I would highly recommend a Caesarean now," the doctor said.

The man and his wife gasped. Layla frowned.

"Doctor, can I speak to you privately for a moment?" Layla asked.

His jaw clenched and he remained silent. She knew the signs. The doctor was pissed off.

At her, of course.

"In the hallway," he said gruffly.

He slid off his purple gloves and tossed them into a makeshift garbage bag she'd set up. He briskly brushed past her and when she entered the hallway with him, she quickly closed the door. He looked up and down the long corridor, most likely to make sure there were no witnesses.

"What the fuck are you doing here?" he hissed in a cold, low voice that should have send shivers of fear down her spine. But she knew this man like the back of her hand. He had never been able to scare her when they'd worked together in the city.

"Working. Same as you," she answered, proud that her voice was as calm as ever.

"If I had known you were working these parts, I would *never* have applied to come out here."

She noted his emphasis on the word never.

"Ditto," she replied. She loved the shock splash across his face.

"About this C-section. Is it one hundred percent necessary? Can we try a natural childbirth first?"

His gaze darkened with anger.

"If you had thought there wasn't a problem you wouldn't have called, now would you? And if you think I'm being spiteful in wanting to cut into a woman, just because I'm pissed at you, think again. Now, are you up to assisting or do I have to get the husband to help?"

Ouch.

"Just make sure you keep your nasty attitude out of the operating room," she retorted.

Instantly she regretted what she had just said. She knew her comment was a low blow and highly unprofessional. He was one of the most qualified doctors she knew, he would never purposely hurt a patient. Even one of hers.

He said nothing as he opened the door and stepped back into the bedroom. She waited in the hallway and took a few calming breaths. The altercation was over. It had been why she had asked to see him privately. So, they could both vent.

She knew without a doubt he would be able to fully concentrate on the task at hand now that they had talked and his thoughts wouldn't be distracted at being dazed in finding her here. Too bad she was still feeling shellshocked at discovering her ex-husband was the local bush doctor. She'd left the city on purpose to come out here and get away from being anywhere near him. She just hoped she would be able to keep her mind on the task at hand.

Layla inhaled a few more breaths in an effort to calm herself. She felt anything but calm as she stepped back inside the bedroom.

• • ⁕ • •

"WHO'S TAKING CARE OF your ranch while you're away?" Brady asked Jenna as she stepped out of her hotel room.

He could tell she'd been crying. Her eyes were red-rimmed and puffy, but he didn't say anything. He had no idea how to console his older sister as he'd never seen her cry before, except when they'd been kids.

They had all agreed to meet outside her motel door at two o'clock sharp and head over to a nearby restaurant for something to eat. Until now, when he needed conversation to distract her, he hadn't even thought to ask about her and Tim's little wilderness ranch.

His question thankfully put a smile to her lips.

"My hermit neighbor. I use him for emergencies. He doesn't like me gone for too long. He's pretty old and set in his routine. He's in his eighties."

Running a ranch was too much work for an older gentleman, in Brady's opinion.

"I think it would be best if I come and help out with the ranch for awhile until we can hire someone." He was surprised when she shook her head.

"Ginny is flying back with me. She said she would stay awhile and help until I can figure something out."

Brady couldn't help but laugh.

"What?" Jenna snapped.

He could tell in the way that the tips of her lips struggled not to curve upward that she knew why he was laughing.

"Oldest sister and youngest sister. You two always fight like cats and dogs."

Jenna grimaced.

"Well, let's hope she's grown up," she retorted.

"Who's grown up?" Ginny suddenly asked from behind them.

Brady and Jenna whirled around to find Ginny and Mitch standing there. Brady expected Jenna to tell Ginny the truth like she always did when they were talking about her. Surprisingly, she didn't.

"No one you know. So, is everyone ready? Remember it's my treat."

There was a chorus of cheers as they all moved along the pathway toward the parking lot.

Gas fumes and the occasional honking from nearby traffic had Brady wishing for the silence of Moose Ranch.

Man, he would give anything to hear the cries of a loon, his daughter's laughter or JJ's voice. He could not wait to get back home. Back to JJ and their baby. And he seriously couldn't wait to meet the newbie kid either.

He smiled inwardly, despite knowing Jenna was going through hell. Guilt at feeling happy at a time like this had him cursing himself for being so cold. He wished like crazy that Tim hadn't died. Wished like hell his sister wasn't experiencing this pain. He had no idea how to soften the blow for her, except to stay with her as long as she needed him.

. . ⚓ . .

RAFE FROWNED AS HE drove his atv into the yard and spied the additional two float planes moored to the dock near their white one. These two planes would account for his earlier suspicions that they might have company. He recognized the yellow one as belonging to the midwife. But he had no clue about the shiny black one.

He left his gear in the trailer, opting to put everything away later. He frowned as he stomped up the stairs and entered the mud room.

He hadn't realized he'd been so tense and full of anxiety for JJ until he heard her laughter float down the hallway. That's when his shoulders slumped and most of the tension left his body.

As he hurried down the hallway he thought he heard a baby crying. But that wasn't possible. JJ still had months to go.

He entered the kitchen and discovered JJ holding what appeared to be a swaddled newborn. Layla held another baby, also swaddled. Both women were rocking each baby as they sat at the kitchen table.

"What the hell is going on here?" he blurted.

# Chapter Eight

Rafe realized his voice sounded quite loud. Too loud for the newborns' ears.

"Sorry," he whispered.

Layla shrugged her shoulders.

"They're going to have to learn to hear loud noises even if they are less than an hour old," she said.

Curiosity shot through him.

"An hour old?"

"Emergency landing. Just like with Blue," JJ explained.

Suddenly he understood and remembered JJ's first winter here at the ranch. They'd had to deliver Blue's baby one night after Kelly had brought her. Blue had been fully in labor.

"The doctor is keeping an eye on the mother in the bedroom down the hall," Layla said.

Rafe nodded and felt he should explain why he'd come home early.

"I tried to get through on the phone but it was busy a few times and then the battery in my phone died. Thought something might have happened here after hearing the planes. So, I cut out on work early."

"Sorry for tying up the line. We needed JJ to make some calls for us after the birth while we used our own phones to call and reschedule our clients," Layla replied.

"We're waiting for the air ambulance now," JJ added, then she refocused her attention to the newborn cradled in her arms. She smiled beautifully at the infant and it made him ache to have their unborn newbie in her arms safe and sound.

He gazed over at the playpen in the living room and was relieved to see Chrissy occupied. She was on her back, reaching with her pudgy arms trying to touch the dancing mobile set over the playpen.

"Is Chrissy hungry?" he enquired.

"She's been fed and changed," JJ replied.

"What can I do to help?" he asked.

"If you wouldn't mind waiting at that airfield you have for the air ambulance and guide them here as quick as possible with a stretcher."

Rafe noted her tight expression and the urgency in Layla's voice and wondered if the mother was okay. He'd ask JJ later.

"Will do. Cute kids," he complimented as he took a moment to gaze at the babies.

Their faces were chubby, their pink rosebud lips were slightly parted as if they might be hungry. Their eyes were closed and framed by long black eyelashes and they looked healthy.

Seconds later he stepped into the late afternoon sunshine and heard the clatter of the helicopter. In the concerned and tense way Layla had appeared, it couldn't get here soon enough.

· · ⌒∞⌒ · ·

JJ STOOD ON THE DOCK, cradling Chrissy and waved as Layla's plane flew skyward. The midwife had stayed back collecting the used medical supplies, other items and JJ had helped her to clean the room. She'd also let Layla know about her pregnancy. Layla had been ecstatic and promised to visit soon so they had more time to talk

Rafe was back in the ranch house preparing dinner, bless his heart.

The air ambulance had taken off several hours ago and the bush doctor had left his plane moored to the dock as he'd accompanied the new father and mother and their newborns to the hospital in Thunder Bay. He'd said he'd be by sometime tomorrow to pick up his plane.

Something interesting she had noticed about Layla and the doctor shortly before the Caesarean. While JJ had been in the kitchen, she'd overheard some not so pleasant words zipping between them while they'd been in the hallway. She hadn't meant to listen in but it would be interesting to find out what was going on between them.

Soon Layla's plane disappeared and JJ focused on the sunset. It was proving to be a beautiful one and she was fascinated by the play of colours as she gazed at the pink and violet tinged puffy white clouds, the pristine blue sky and a beaver splashing its wide tail against the pinkish purple shaded waves about twenty feet away.

Chrissy giggled with every loud splash of the beaver's tail and kept reaching up to pull off her sun bonnet, but it didn't budge thanks to it being tied beneath her chin. JJ grinned and wondered how long it would take before she figured out how to untie it.

The wind picked up and it turned cooler as the sun disappeared beneath the silhouette of the black forest toward the west shore of the lake. Spooky shadows danced all around and the lonesome cries of the loons sliced through the air.

"Okay, sweetie. Time for supper. You must be hungry," JJ said as she hugged her daughter to her chest.

The baby smiled up at JJ.

"Ahh, sweetie. You are just so beautiful. I cannot even imagine my life without you in it. You are the best thing that ever happened to me," she whispered as they headed up the path to the ranch house.

And the guys are also the best thing that happened. And our little unborn baby, she added.

She thought she felt the slightest little fluttering in her womb and wondered if the baby knew she was talking about her or him, or was it just her wishful thinking? Was the baby going to be a girl? Or a boy? Were there going to be complications like what happened with Tita? She'd only been able to give her a quick goodbye hug as they'd taken her out of the room on a stretcher. She'd still looked deathly pale but she'd appeared happy. Her husband had looked worried.

JJ frowned. What if something *did* go wrong during her own labor? But what if everything went right?

JJ hugged Chrissy tighter. JJ felt so lucky with her family but how long before her luck ran out, like Jenna's luck had run out with her husband?

As she entered the ranch house, an array of aromas greeted her, chasing away her thoughts. Thankfully, her morning sickness had left hours ago and the spices and frying onions and steak made her mouth water.

"It smells perfect," JJ laughed as she carried Chrissy into the kitchen. Rafe stood at the stove, wearing her apron and an awesome smile.

"Steak, onions, mashed potatoes and a Caesar salad at your service," he said and his gaze drew to Chrissy, who was now squirming in her arms with delight. Rafe"s brown eyes twinkled merrily.

"And for you, I've got some mashed potatoes, mashed steak and squished peas."

Chrissy gave out an excited squeal as JJ placed her in the highchair.

"Rafe, you cooked, so I'll serve," she volunteered.

He shook his head.

"Baby, you've been through a lot today. You take a load off and let me serve my two beautiful women."

*His two beautiful women.* JJ liked that Rafe considered Chrissy as his own. It made them one big happy family.

"Dan called. He won't be back tonight. Found a couple of dead cattle. Figured it could be the wolf pack he saw. He's going to scout around. Says he should be back by supper tomorrow."

JJ nodded as she quickly wiped down Chrissy's hands with a warm soapy cloth.

"I'll just wash up. Back in a minute," she said.

"I'll keep an eye on Chrissy. She may try to escape her highchair due to the fact vegetables are on her menu," Rafe teased.

JJ laughed and hurried down the hall to the bathroom. She quickly tended to her needs and then washed her face and hands and then she caught her reflection in the mirror. Her cheeks were rosy and her eyes were sparkly like little diamonds were in them. She looked healthy.

Today had turned out to be a good day, even with her unexpected guests. She was thrilled the doctor had been able to save the babies and the mother. All had worked out. Maybe she was reading too much into her doom and gloom thinking?

Her thoughts turned to Dan who would be camping in a rustic cabin tonight. What kind of food had he packed for himself? Was he hungry?

What about Brady? She hadn't heard from him all day. She wondered where he was tonight. She hoped Jenna found comfort in having her siblings with her.

JJ inhaled deeply and blew out a calming breath. Life was so weird. One minute someone you loved was there and then they were gone.

She shook off the dreadful thoughts and left the bathroom. She wanted to hold on to this good feeling for a while longer because things never stayed the same for long.

· · ∽ · ·

THREE HOURS LATER, Rafe and JJ lay cradled in each others' arms in his bed.

After dinner, he'd showered and she'd spent time playing with Chrissy. When Rafe had returned, he'd played with her and then she'd showered. They'd put Chrissy down to sleep a little while ago and then they'd cleaned up the kitchen, where she'd explained to him what had happened today. He'd become quiet, his cheerfulness gone. He was still quiet now while they lay in bed and it worried her.

"What's wrong?" she asked as she snuggled closer to his strong warm body.

"Thinking," he said softly and kissed her left cheek.

"About?" she prodded.

"The newbie."

"Are you afraid the baby might be yours?" she blurted, remembering the forlorn expression on his face the other night during dinner, after she'd announced her pregnancy.

"God, no, I am not afraid of the kid being mine. I hope newbie is mine. I'd love to father a baby for you," he said and held her tighter to him.

His confession brought a rush of relief and excitement.

"Then why are you so quiet tonight?"

"You should have newbie in the hospital," he announced.

"But—"

"Now hear me out. Look what happened to that lady today. You said there were complications and Layla had to call in the doctor. What would have happened if the doctor hadn't gotten here in time?"

"But he did."

"JJ, what if he *didn't* get here on time?" Rafe sighed and held her tighter. Muscles jerked in his cheeks and she realized he was seriously upset.

"If you think I don't have doubts, then you'd have to call me crazy," she admitted.

A smile whispered across his lips.

"I don't want anything bad to happen to you or the baby."

JJ nodded. "I understand."

"So we'll go to the hospital near your due date?"

His gaze was so hopeful that she wished she could make him happy with her decision. But it was *her* decision.

"Despite our fears. I need to be here at home with all my guys around me. I want Chrissy here too when the baby is born."

"Sweetie, what if..."

JJ reached up and placed her fingertips on his lips.

"Rafe, seriously, you're starting to think like me. Please, don't. I need your confidence as my shelter. I know I'm asking a lot to put your fears aside for me, especially when I'm having so much trouble doing it myself."

His brow furrowed and he stared at her.

"Has your anxiety returned?" he asked.

"Tim's death has rattled me. I had a panic attack on the way back the other day after dropping off Brady and Mitch, so I did an emergency landing. The attack was followed by a bad bout of morning sickness. Lucas got crackers and ginger ale from his cabin and brought them out to me. I felt better afterward."

"Who is this guy? This Lucas?" he asked, a scowl on his face.

"He's a newfound friend. He saw me land and he came in his motorboat looking to see if I was in trouble."

"A knight in shining armor in a motorboat," he grumbled.

JJ giggled.

"Are you jealous?"

"Damn right. I want to be your knight in shining armor."

"You do, eh?"

His scowl disappeared and she realized he'd been teasing her.

"Yeah, I do."

"Then be my knight and make love to me," she whispered, feeling all tingly happy as his hot mouth slid over hers.

JJ opened her mouth and Rafe's hot tongue plunged between her teeth. Their tongues met in a duel of passion. Her head spun with excitement at the impact and every intimate nerve ending in her body sparkled to life. She moaned her approval and struggled to get closer to him. She slapped her hands upon his bare shoulders, her fingers digging into his hard, smooth muscles.

His kiss intensified.

Exquisite tension quickly mounted as his hand smoothed over her abdomen. His work-calloused palm and long fingers caressed her sensitive flesh, moving in slow sultry circles toward the apex of her thighs.

He kissed her harder, and her body hummed with anticipation as his fingers moved against her swollen clitoris. She whimpered into his mouth when he touched her clit. He began a tortuously seductive massage over the sensitive bundle of nerves, making her arch against him. Delicious sensations assaulted her and fevered heat raced through her.

Suddenly Rafe broke the kiss and pulled his head away. As he gazed at her, his brown eyes blazed with a raging need just as fierce as hers.

"How's that for a knight in shining armor?" he breathed heavily; his smile crooked.

"Oh, baby. You can be my knight anytime," JJ gasped.

Her voice sounded thick and aroused, her senses very aware that her pussy was throbbing and her vagina was already dripping with her cream.

"Keep doing what you're doing and please don't hold back. The baby is fine, I promise," she murmured, moving even closer. She licked his moist lips.

"Take me, sweetheart. Do with me what you wish," he said with a chuckle and made no more moves to arouse her.

Damn him! He'd lit the passion inside of her and now he was giving her the reins.

Well, she could give just as good as she got! And she knew he wouldn't last long under her tutelage, because when she was on fire, she couldn't hold back.

She wrapped her arms around his neck and kissed him. She possessed his mouth so brutally that he groaned and she answered with a whimper. She rubbed her breasts against his chest, loving how his rough chest hairs excited her nipples, making them rigid and hurt so good.

She felt the heavy, hot outline of his shaft against her thigh. Felt it growing and jerking as she rubbed her leg against his rigid flesh. She lifted her leg over his thigh and pressed her clitoris against his cock, rubbing and gyrating on him. Pleasure came quickly and her body tightened, readying for a climax.

Rafe must have sensed it for he groaned and slid his hands onto her hips. He held her tight and without breaking the kiss, he lifted her and brought her over him and then down upon him.

She gasped as his cock conquered her vagina, sliding into her, long and thick. Deep and hot. In seconds, she was straddling him, undulating, causing an erotic friction against her clitoris. The flares of pleasure ignited.

His hands slid between their bodies and he cupped her breasts, his thumbs rubbing her nipples until she exploded like a bomb.

She went wild on his shaft, completely electrified as her wet vagina muscles clenched his velvet-encased solid flesh. She shattered beneath the erotic waves that washed over her in dark currents and bucked as the flames consumed her.

She tore her mouth from his and cried out his name, gasping for air as the pleasure flew around her like a tornado. She was burning and loving the shudders and the convulsions. They just kept coming and she was going to ride the inferno for as long as she could.

. . ⚓ . .

RAFE GRINNED AS HE watched. Her eyes were scrunched tight and her mouth open into an O as she rode him. Her body was arching and her breasts were bouncing beneath his hands as she frantically undulated upon his cock. His shaft throbbed and thickened painfully inside her, under her sensually torturous assault but he was completely enthralled by her sexy moans and her submissive whimpers.

Her climax was hard and long and he sensed the pleasure was consuming her. It's where she wanted to be. Free and flying.

He rocked against her, meeting her gyrations with his own. When he sensed she was nearing the end, he let go of his self control, gasping as the carnal tremors shot through to his very core.

He pumped upward with uncontrollable thrusts and within seconds the lightning bolts of his climax shot through his cock and balls and spiralled into his belly, making him shoot his seed deep inside of her.

・・ ◈ ・・

THE EARLY MORNING SUN was already high in the sky as JJ waved goodbye to Rafe when he drove the atv out of the nearby shed and passed her and Chrissy as they stood in the front yard of the ranch house. After last night's lovemaking, they'd both slept through the night, only to be awoken by Chrissy, who was crying in her crib.

Rafe had joked she was a good alarm clock and they had both grabbed their robes and hurried to get her. She'd calmed down when JJ had swept her out of her crib. After cleaning and changing her, she'd given her daughter breakfast. The poor dear had been famished and ate everything JJ fed her. By the time Rafe had finished his shower and dressed, she'd had bacon, eggs and pancakes with Brady's homemade maple syrup whipped up for both of them.

Thankfully, no morning sickness and she enjoyed her meal. While they hurriedly ate, they discussed where he'd be working today and then when they'd finished breakfast they'd put together a healthy lunch of submarine sandwiches for him and a few canned items to carry along for emergency food.

Then her knight was gone and she and Chrissy were alone again.

But not for long because the instant the rumble of Rafe's vehicle faded away; it was replaced by the low purr of an airplane coming in from the north.

"I bet you I know who that is. I bet you it's the young bush doctor who was here yesterday to come and pick up his plane," JJ said to Chrissy.

Chrissy paid her no attention as her gaze flew to the sky and they watched a yellow floatplane soar into view overhead and then it swept down and landed in the lake with a splash.

A yellow plane meant Layla, and JJ was thrilled her midwife was back so soon. When they reached the dock, JJ noticed that the doctor had come along with Layla.

And boy, in the way he was yanking on the ropes while he tied down her plane, he did appear pissed off. It also looked like Layla was ignoring him as she stood at the end of the dock.

She wore white running shoes, navy blue slacks and matching long sleeved blue top, which was her traditional midwife uniform and her black midwife tote bag was slung over one shoulder. Her arms were crossed over her chest as she gazed out across the glass-like lake.

This morning there wasn't so much as a breeze and the air smelled of sun-baked pine needles. The sky was cloudless and a brilliant baby blue. She sensed it was going to be another hot, sunny day like yesterday.

"Good morning!" JJ called out to them as she stepped onto the dock with a quiet Chrissy who gazed curiously at the doctor.

The doctor said nothing but threw them a wave as he now hurriedly untied his own plane from the mooring.

At JJ's greeting, Layla whirled around, her curly dark brown shoulder length hair bouncing. For a moment, a spear of concern shot through JJ as she caught a very unhappy look on Layla's face,

Oh dear, she hoped that nothing bad had happened to Tita or her babies. But Layla immediately recovered with a genuine smile and JJ sensed Layla's gloom might have something to do with the doctor.

"Good morning, right back at you two!" Layla called out with a friendly wave to them.

Chrissy's feet began to kick wildly with excitement.

"I just put on a fresh pot of coffee and I've got orange pecan cookies. You are both welcome to join me."

She'd removed the homemade cookies from one of their freezers last night, where she always kept a bunch on hand for her cowboys. And of course she'd snuck some into Rafe's lunch bag. He would be pleasantly surprised.

Just thinking of Rafe put a smile in her heart and for a brief second she remembered their lovemaking last night, with her falling asleep on top of him, his cock buried deep inside of her. She'd slept on him like that all night and she swore she'd slept harder than any night since coming here.

"Sorry, JJ. I've got patients this morning. I'll have to take a rain check!" the doctor shouted.

"Okay, rain check. You are welcome here anytime. And how about you, Layla? Fresh coffee and cookies?"

"Would love some. Thank you. It'll give me a chance to visit with Miss. Chrissy. May I hold her?" Layla asked as she joined them. Her bright brown eyes were looking quite cheerful now.

"Of course, you may."

JJ handed the baby to Layla, who hugged her close.

"You have grown, Little Miss. Your mommy and daddy are taking very good care of you."

"She's a beautiful baby," the doctor commented.

JJ detected extreme desolation in his eyes as he watched Layla interact with Chrissy. And her heart clenched too with empathy for him. Had he had some sort of heartbreak in his past?

When he noticed JJ watching him, he looked away and quickly entered his bush plane. In the doorway, he turned and called out with a wave.

"Thanks for yesterday! It was greatly appreciated. Just so you know, mother and kids are doing great!"

Before she could respond, he slammed the door shut.

"Sorry, about his gruffness. We had an argument on the plane," Layla explained as she began walking along the dock.

"I hope nothing too serious," JJ commented.

"He hates me."

Her confession rocked JJ.

"Oh dear, I'm so sorry."

Layla shook her head.

"Don't be. I hate him too. I'll tell you over coffee what's going on."

Curiosity shifted through JJ. Layla had used the hate word. There was a very fine line between hate and love, which made her believe there *was* something besides hate going on between doctor and midwife.

"You are so cute!" Layla said and snuggled her cheek against Chrissy's cheek and her daughter giggled.

When they reached the ranch house, Layla played with Chrissy while JJ poured the coffee into mugs. And then she placed the mugs and a plate of cookies onto the dining room table. She watched as Layla interacted with Chrissy, making funny faces at her until she was laughing hysterically. With Layla's antics and Chrissy being happy, it really brightened JJ's mood.

Huh, she hadn't even realized she'd been feeling a little sad after watching Rafe leave, until just now.

Hormones. It had to be.

Layla played with her daughter a little while longer and then placed her into her playpen. To JJ surprise, Chrissy's eyes fluttered closed and she was fast asleep.

"Wow, you do have a way with kids," JJ commented after they sat down.

"Kids are a passion of mine," Layla said as she picked up a cookie and took a bite.

"Hey, these are really good."

"Thanks. The guys love them too."

Layla chuckled.

"I bet. And poor silly Willie, doesn't know what he's missing," Layla replied and munched on the cookie. She closed her eyes and made moaning sounds of appreciation.

From outside came the roar of the doctor's bush plane as he started it.

"Just so you know, Willie's my ex-husband and he can't stand the sight of me and I can't stand the sight of him. One of us is going to have to leave these parts, and it sure isn't going to be me," Layla said with a frown.

# Chapter Nine

JJ felt her mouth drop open in shock. The midwife and the doctor had been married.

"Sorry, I guess I shouldn't be airing my dirty laundry to my client. Anyways, we parted on not friendly terms. He's still not friendly and neither am I with him. And that's the way it will stay until he's gone."

Layla's eyes flashed with anger and her cheeks were flushed. She placed her hands upon the table and smiled at JJ.

"So, let's talk about you and that is why I'm here, aside from offering Willie a ride over. I had hoped to talk him into leaving, but he is a stubborn man and here I am on the subject of him again. My apologies."

"I am just so sorry you are going through this turmoil. He seemed like a nice fellow," JJ commented. Although she had thought he'd been harsh with Layla yesterday in the hallway during that conversation she'd overheard prior to the Caesarean. But he did appear to take his work very seriously as Tita and her babies were alive.

Layla sighed.

"Well, he was nice. Actually our marriage was really nice. That is, until we hit a really bad speed bump. But I can't go into it. He is a great doctor though. While we were together we talked about working in the north. It came as a shock that he decided on practicing in the same area as I'm practicing in. If I didn't know he hated me so much, I would think he's here to torment me on purpose."

"He did appear miserable earlier so I don't think he's here on purpose," JJ soothed.

"Yeah, well, I don't know. He used to be an easygoing man and not the tenacious oaf he is now. Anyways, thank goodness for these delicious cookies and coffee. Consider them stress eating," she said with a giggle and grabbed a third cookie. Her eyes closed and she moaned again as she bit it.

JJ suddenly had this overwhelming urge to help Dr. Willie and Layla, but she had no idea how.

"Hey, you know you can tell me anything. If you need to vent, I am here for you. Not only am I your client, but I am also your friend," JJ offered.

Layla appeared to relax. She inhaled deeply; her shoulders slumped. She took a huge gulp of coffee and helped herself to a fourth cookie.

"You are so sweet, JJ. But no need for venting at the moment. I did give Willie a piece of my mind on the plane. And I must tell you, it felt good," Layla said with a laugh.

"And I was so thrilled when you told me you were pregnant again," she continued. "I could barely sleep last night. Were you and Brady trying to get pregnant or was this a surprise, if I can ask?"

"It was a surprise," JJ admitted.

"And I assume you two already saw your doctor?" she asked as she reached into her bag and brought out a pad of paper and a pen.

JJ nodded. She didn't elaborate that she'd gone to see her doctor in secret.

"And how far along are you?"

"She said it appears almost three months with a due date of December 25."

Layla burst out laughing and clutched her hands to her chest. Her brown eyes glittered with happiness.

"Again? That was the same due date as Chrissy, wasn't it?" she squealed.

"I was just as surprised as you are," JJ admitted.

"I bet. And how is Brady reacting, having another baby so close together?"

JJ bit her bottom lip. How in the world could she respond to that question?

"By the look on your face, he's not happy?" Layla asked.

JJ swallowed. Maybe it was time to confide in Layla? Tell her about how things worked around here. In the bedroom.

"Oh, he was quite surprised at first but now he's happy. But whatever I tell you is only between you and I, right? Confidential?"

A serious expression flittered across Layla's face.

"Of course. I never repeat what a client tells me, unless she gives me permission to do so, and only under the direst of circumstances. Anything you say to me is safe. I'm like a vault." She made a zipper motion with her finger over her mouth.

Okay. Maybe it was time to confide in Layla.

"I don't know who the baby's father is," she blurted. There, it was out and for a few seconds, Layla just blinked. No surprise. No shock. Just blank and blink.

*Boy, she has a good poker face.*

"That's fine. There are ways you can find out. I would suggest waiting until after the baby is born. But, if you can't wait."

"Oh, we can wait. We want to do whatever is safe for the baby."

"Well, it's entirely up to you."

To JJ's surprise, Layla didn't ask who the father might be.

But her voice lowered as if she didn't want anyone overhearing.

"Does Brady know?"

"Yes, he knows."

"And he's okay with this. Not knowing if he's the father. I mean, it's none of my business. But I want to make sure you're safe here. I mean, he doesn't seem like the jealous type or the violent kind or—"

"Oh, God, no. I should tell you we have an open relationship."

JJ was met with the poker face again. Layla just blinked at her.

"Are you okay? More stress?" JJ asked her as Layla suddenly grabbed for another cookie.

She shook her head, which made her curly hair bounce.

"I'm fine, and no judgement from me. I've heard a lot of things from my clients. I am a midwife and I have made it my policy to remain neutral and I only offer help if asked. You and Brady have an open relationship. He's okay with maybe not being the dad. I am assuming the other man knows about the baby? And your open relationship? And he isn't the jealous or violent type?"

"He does and he's okay with it too." JJ held back that there were two other men involved and not just one other one. But she'd keep that part quiet. It just might be too much information for Layla to handle.

Her midwife was watching her carefully now and amazement was flashing in her eyes.

"I'm so proud of you, JJ. It sounds like you've got everything under control."

Now it was JJ's turn to blink with shock. Layla was proud of her? She had everything under control? A tinge of anxiety and desperation grabbed a hold.

"Actually no, I don't have everything under control. That's my problem. There is something I really need to discuss with you," JJ bit out.

A furrow of concern erupted between Layla's eyebrows.

"Hon, you can tell me anything, especially after what you've already confided. We are now kindred spirits."

And then, just like that, all of JJ's worries came pouring out like a festering wound.

"I've been experiencing a lot of anxiety. Fear of terrible things happening. I thought I had a good handle on my anxiety, especially after the post partum blues went away. The anxiety pops up now and again but I was able to manage it. But it got much worse all of a sudden, especially after the unexpected death of Brady's sister's husband a few days ago. That's why he's not here. He's gone to Tim's funeral and I miss him terribly and he might stay away a long time to help out his sister. The guys are taking on extra work and I worry about them, about bad things happening to them. What if this happens? What if that happens? About dreadful things happening to Chrissy and myself."

Layla reached out and placed a hand over JJ's hand. The gesture suddenly brought JJ back to the present.

"Shh, it's going to be fine. Let me tell you a few things about pregnant women. But first, my condolences to Brady and his sister and her family. I'm sorry to hear this. You said it happened unexpectedly. I bet you were shocked."

"Very shocked. We all were. The phone call came early in the morning and that's always a bad sign, am I right? Since then, my anxiety has been through the roof. Except yesterday and today. I was so distracted; I didn't have time to freak out, but I just know when I have time to think, I'll start to worry again and then my mind will race and the anxiety will come back. Anyways I don't like his feeling of doom and gloom. It's going to ruin what should be a happy time for me."

Layla nodded and sipped her coffee.

JJ continued.

"I even had to put down my plane the other day. Due to a panic attack. And I hyperventilated and then my morning sickness kicked in big time and I felt so sad because I couldn't control any of it."

"Okay, let me tell you something about pregnant women," she said softly.

"It's all about the hormones. Of course, you are more anxious while you are pregnant. Did you know that when a woman is pregnant, her hormones actually change her brain? She becomes alert to signs of threats. It's so you can protect your baby. Did you know that in general the area of the brain that processes fear and anger are larger in a woman than in a man, even before she is pregnant? And since you're already predisposed to anxiety due to your past, does it not make sense that you are reacting? Your reactions are all normal. Sure, it doesn't feel good, but it is just hormones. It is your body's way of protecting your unborn baby. Just don't grab hold to the anxiety. Don't let it consume you. Let it wash over you. Tell yourself as many times as it takes for the emotions you don't want to feel to go away."

"Oh, is that all?" JJ joked.

Layla smiled.

"Well, I could get more technical if you like?"

JJ shook her head.

"No, it's okay. I'll just digest what you've told me."

"Did you know that a woman also has an extra helping of emotions compared to men? That is why we are quite emotional when pregnant, even in the best of times. Sad, happy, everything in between. It's hormones and hormones are here to help protect your offspring. It ensures the survival of the human race. And do you know what? There's something else, women's instincts are also known to be more robust in the brain than men. And do you know what the good news is?"

"There's good news?"

Layla nodded.

"Yes, there's always good news, no matter how bad something seems. Our brains are always changing and now I am talking about us in general even when we are not pregnant. This pertains to men also. Studies have shown our brain can grow new patterns and pathways. It's something called neuroplasticity. Look it up on the internet when you get a chance. You can retrain your brain simply by changing the way you *feel*. Our thoughts are what makes us feel good or bad. In neuroplasticity you imagine how you want to feel. Don't judge yourself when you feel bad and don't have unrealistic expectations. Anytime you find your thoughts slipping toward worrying, which in turn can produce your anxiety, imagine how you want to *feel* instead. The brain will listen to your thoughts because your thoughts are orders. It takes a lot of work, but work is certainly worth it if your goal is to feel better, right?"

"Easier said than done," JJ admitted.

She had been trying to change her way of thinking and she'd had some success. But this setback was just so unnerving. It made her believe that she would never get better. But Layla had just said to let the feelings ride through her and not to judge herself. And to make herself feel what she *wanted* to feel.

Layla had to be right, especially about the hormones causing her anxiety to increase. She was a midwife. She'd studied this stuff.

"Let me give you an example. Before and during your training, did you doubt you would ever become a pilot?" Layla asked.

"Yes, many times," JJ agreed.

"You've told me about your anxiety and panic attack issues during our prior meetings, so I know when you want to do something, it may not be as easy for you as it would be for someone who doesn't have anxiety. My point is, you were able to get your pilot license because you were able to retrain your brain into believing you could do it and despite your anxiety, you pushed through it, even though it felt bad. Am I right?"

"Bad is an understatement. But, yes, I did it." Pride bubbled through JJ. She'd been a nervous wreck, shaking and trembling, her tummy somersaulting with nausea and thoughts of backing out every time her teacher splashed down onto the lake in her plane to give her a lesson.

But she'd made it through because she'd wanted it bad enough. Up until her last plane trip, she'd enjoyed soaring into the sky, but now her confidence was shattered with the what if she had another panic attack when she flew again.

"You've already got a head start over plenty of people who have anxiety and panic disorder. Because you've researched how to change your way of thinking. You knew it wasn't going to change overnight.

But you persevered. You knew the more you practiced your new way of thinking, the stronger those pathways of positive thinking become in the brain and the weaker the older pathways with anxiety become. Make sense? So homework for you. Study all you can about neuroplasticity, JJ. Learn how to make those new connections in the brain get even stronger. I did and I can tell you from my experience it works."

"You've had anxiety issues as well?" Wow, this was big news.

Layla frowned and sighed heavily. Suddenly she looked very sad and JJ wished she hadn't asked that question.

"It was more of a grief issue for me. I couldn't get the traditional ways to help me. You know grief group therapy, a shrink. My grief was something I really needed to get over and neuroplasticity showed me the way. But the grief is something I don't like to talk about. I prefer to stay in the here and now and be positive," she said softly.

JJ's heart went out to the woman and she wondered what had happened. But she didn't dare ask. Layla had said she didn't want to talk about it.

Then Layla brightened.

"JJ, anytime you need to reach out to me you have my pager number. Even if you need me to talk or discuss your anxiety or whatever is happening to cause it, just feel free to call. Sometimes I may not be able to call back right away as I may be with a patient, but just call my pager. I keep it with me all the time. As you said, I am not only your midwife, I am also your friend."

Relief blew through JJ like a tornado. That she could talk to a friend about this anxiety was really helpful.

"That would be really nice. Thank you so much."

Layla beamed.

"Not a problem. Now, I'd like to take your vitals and we can discuss prenatal vitamins...that is if your family doctor didn't already prescribe them?"

"No, I told her I was going with my same midwife again. So I am in your capable hands."

"Awesome! Okay, let's get started before Chrissy wakes up."

JJ nodded. Suddenly she felt stronger having someone in her corner to talk to. Maybe everything was going to be alright after all.

.. ⚘ ..

"THAT WAS A NICE FUNERAL for Tim," Brady commented as he and Mitch entered the hotel room they shared.

"They did a good job pulling it together at such short notice," Mitch replied as he set his chocolate milkshake, burger and french fries down on the night table between their beds. Then he removed his shoes and sat on the bed.

Concern rolled through Brady as he sat on the other bed and eyed the food.

"I meant to ask you earlier, but the girls were around. Should you be eating that kind of stuff? Didn't you have a heart attack issue?" Brady enquired.

Mitch chuckled and shrugged his shoulders.

"Hey, man. The heart attack was stress related. I'm not stressed anymore. And once in awhile, having some junk food won't kill me. Besides, I need it to cheer me up. I miss home."

Brady nodded. He missed his ranch too. Missed the peace. His daughter and the newbie. JJ. The guys. The forest. The meadows. His cattle.

"Me too," Brady admitted. "But at least the ones we love are at home waiting for us. Jenna has nobody at home. He's in that casket in the ground."

Beside him, Mitch visibly shivered.

"Yeah, a cold bed for him tonight," Mitch said. "I'm going to try and talk her into selling her ranch. With Tim gone, it's going to be too much for her."

"She said that Ginny was going to move in for awhile until she could find some help," Brady answered.

Brady wasn't surprised when Mitch started to laugh. He laughed hard. A roar deep from his belly and then he closed his eyes and kept laughing, slapping his knees and pushing his back up against the headboard.

Brady shook his head. He grinned at his brother and took the opportunity to sneak a sip of Mitch's delicious chocolate milkshake and a couple of his salty fries

"Hey, I saw that." Mitch complained as he recovered and opened his eyes.

Brady grinned and chewed on the fries.

"Something I guess I should tell you. Just keep it under your hat for now, okay?" Brady said.

Mitch frowned.

"Sounds serious."

"It is. JJ is pregnant, again."

Mitch swore softly, but his expression brightened.

"Wow, You guys are going to have a dozen kids in no time flat in the way you're going."

Brady nodded.

"But, you don't look happy," Mitch pointed out.

"Oh, I am. Just worried I guess. I want the kid to be healthy." *And I want to know that I am the father*, he added silently.

"Man, that's so cool. That means I'm going to be an uncle again. Wait until I tell Milena. She is going to be so excited."

So much for Mitch keeping the news under his hat for now.

"Milena is a good woman. I can tell," Brady praised. "She's a hard worker too. I like what she's done with your vegetable garden."

Mitch beamed.

"She tends to it every day and she spends her days off working in it too."

"JJ does the same with our garden. She's a gem," Brady replied.

"So is Milena," Mitch added happily and he began chowing down his burger and sipping on his milkshake.

From the ecstatic expression on Mitch's face, Brady knew his brother had found his forever girl. And although he and Mitch hadn't had the discussion, JJ had told him that the three men were sharing Milena.

He also knew that if Mitch wanted to share Milena with Paul and Daegen, then that was Mitch's business. Just like sharing JJ with Rafe and Dan was his own business. No one else needed to know their arrangement.

But he sure wished he knew if he was the biological father.

•• ⌘ ••

THE SUDDEN DISAPPEARANCE of the sun overhead had Rafe switching off the tractor. He lifted his cowboy hat off his head and welcomed the hot wind as it cooled his sweat-drenched face and hair. He'd worked straight through lunch and hadn't noticed the change in weather until just now.

Gazing upward, he spied the dark anvil-shaped thunderhead clouds amassing quickly overhead.

Shit. He should have checked the weather forecast, but he'd been too busy to bother. Sure, he could have listened to the radio last night while they'd been washing the dishes. But he'd been busy chatting with JJ about Tita. Or he could have listened this morning during breakfast, but they'd gotten up so late and he'd hurried to leave wanting to catch up due to his stopping work early yesterday.

He inhaled deeply as he remembered awakening to find JJ fast asleep on him. Had the kid not been crying, he would have taken JJ right then and there again. He winced as his cock pulsed as he remembered how tightly her vaginal muscles were wrapped around his shaft, like it belonged inside of her. Like they fit together.

He wished like crazy he was back at the house right now making sure she was alright. He hoped Dan had returned. Hoped she wouldn't get scared because of this storm.

A silver fork of lightning blazed through the black clouds. Thunder immediately crackled, sending a cord of urgency through him.

Time to make camp and wait this out. It would be too dangerous to head back to the ranch house now. This storm was erupting quite quickly and he'd be a moving target for lightning if he didn't take cover.

He switched on the tractor and drove to where he'd parked his atv at the far end of the meadow. In a few minutes, he had the lightning proof tent out of the knapsack he stored beneath the tarp in the trailer.

He moved quickly, setting the tent far from the vehicles and the trees, and in a bit of a hollow in case of lightning strikes. The ground he picked was also slightly sloped, so water would drain away during downpours.

He carried the cooler and sleeping bag to the pitched tent, made sure he had the phone with him, and slipped inside to await the storm.

. . ⚓ . .

LAYLA HAD LEFT HOURS ago and after Chrissy had awoken, JJ had given her a snack and then they'd spent the rest of the morning outside. JJ, working in the vegetable garden while musing over her conversation with Layla. Chrissy, playing with her toys in the portable playpen, which JJ had set beneath the shade of a nearby pine tree.

The creepy grumble of thunder had her packing them both up, abandoning the portable playpen where it was and heading into the ranch house. Upon entering, she heard the phone ringing and hurried to grab it.

"Moose Ranch, happy stormy afternoon!" she said cheerfully as she placed Chrissy in her highchair.

"Glad I caught you."

JJ instantly became alert at Rafe's tense voice.

"Going to be a delay in coming home. This storm looks bad. Getting really windy here and I think there will be trees down. So don't worry about me."

There was a silence, and for a moment she thought she had lost him.

"...Dan, yet?" he said. She hadn't heard the first part of the sentence.

"Can you repeat that, Rafe. Bad connection."

"Yeah...did you hear from Dan yet? Did he get back there yet?"

She glanced at the answering machine. The light was not blinking, indicating no messages.

Why hadn't Dan called? It was after lunch time. Had something happened to him?

"No, nothing."

"He's probably out of range and hunkered down to wait out the storm. I'll try calling him and you again later. Everything good there?"

JJ nodded as she stared at the back living room window. The pine trees were really swaying and it was getting very dark. Nervousness crawled through her.

"Everything is fine. Layla was by to visit and the doctor picked up his plane."

"Those must have been the planes I heard. How is the kid? Has she been eating?"

"Yes. I'm sticking to her favorites."

JJ frowned as static crackled on the phone.

"...can't hear you," she heard him say.

"Where exactly are you?" she asked.

Her grip tightened on the phone as bright lightning flashed at the dark windows.

Suddenly, the line went dead.

# Chapter Ten

Another ominous crackle of thunder reminded JJ she'd left some of the windows open for fresh air. Hurriedly, she grabbed Chrissy from the highchair and placed her into the safety of the playpen in the middle of the living room, then she rushed around, closing the downstairs windows.

As she shut the guest bedroom windows, she peered outside and watched her daughter's play pen fly off the ground and crash into some nearby bushes. Her gut hollowed out at the frightening sight. Then a silver wall of rain slammed against the panes barring the view.

*The upstairs windows are open too!*

Her heart pounded like crazy as she raced upstairs and ran around closing the windows. The shrieking wind and the rain pounding the sheet metal roof made it seem like her entire world was exploding. She tried to force herself to remain calm and was thankful it hadn't gotten wet upstairs because the house had large overhangs.

As she closed the last window, a flash of lightning illuminated the silvery sheets of rain and an ear-splitting shatter of thunder crashed through the room, making JJ scream as she ran back into the hallway.

From the first floor, Chrissy began to cry.

"Mommy is coming, sweet cheeks!" she called out.

She trembled as she imagined the roof flying off and the wind sucking her out, leaving Chrissy all alone.

Her legs felt weak as she held herself back from running down the stairs. The last thing she wanted was to fall down the steps and break her neck, leaving her daughter without a mother.

Thankfully, when Chrissy saw her rushing into the living room, she stopped crying. JJ scooped her up and wiped away the tears streaming down her pink cheeks. There was a frightened pout on her cupid bow shaped lips and her blue eyes, wide with fear, darted from window to window as the rain bombarded the main floor windowpanes.

There were times like these she wished they didn't have so many windows. What if one of them broke? And the storm came inside?

JJ caught her spiralling thoughts and focused her attention to her daughter, who snuggled warmly against her. But she still looked scared.

"It's okay. It's just a storm," JJ reassured in as calm a voice as she could muster. She bounced Chrissy and forced herself to smile, despite wanting to cry instead.

She jumped as the phone rang.

Heavens! The phone was already back?

"This better be Dan," she said a little too loudly as she picked up the receiver and spoke.

Static was her answer.

The wind continued to howl. Lightning flashed at the windows and a devastating crack of thunder immediately followed making the floorboards tremble beneath her feet.

Chrissy began to cry again.

She was about to hang up the phone when she heard Dan's voice.

"Can you hear me? It's Dan."

*Oh, Thank God.*

"Everything okay, Dan?"

Static.

Shoot! She wanted to confess to him that she was getting really scared. But if he was calling, it meant he wasn't coming home at the moment, so she needed to keep it together and show a brave front.

Then she heard him again.

"Bad wind, JJ. Can you hear me?"

"Yes! Yes, I hear you. It is windy here too!"

"Bad storm. Trees are going to be down on the trail. Won't be back tonight. I'm staying at Misty Lake cabin! Is Rafe back?" He was shouting and he didn't sound in the least bit scared.

Wow. Must be nice to be like that.

"Rafe is at number six. In his tent," she yelled back.

She hoped he could hear her.

Silence.

"Dan! Can you hear me?"

Nothing. The line was dead again.

*Seriously?*

JJ slammed the receiver down and her nervousness began to spin its ugly web around her. What if a tornado comes and rips the house apart? What if something bad happens to one of the guys?

*Damn! Calm down! Nothing is going to happen! Yeah right. It's Armageddon out there!*

Dan and Rafe had weathered plenty of storms. They would be fine. If the wind got worse, she and Chrissy would just hunker down in the basement.

More bright flashes of lightning. Another shattering crack of thunder.

Chrissy cried louder.

"It's okay. It's okay. It's just thunder. It can't hurt us."

It had gotten so dark, she decided to turn on the lights. Then she could put on something to eat and play the radio.

She flipped on the nearby switch.

Nothing happened. The power was out.

*Shoot!*

Sometimes the generator kicked in automatically, but one of the guys must have taken it off standby for some reason. She'd have to go outside to get one of the generators going, but there was no way she was going out in this.

"Man, what I wouldn't give to have the radio blasting about now," JJ murmured and kissed Chrissy's wet cheeks.

But they were fresh out of batteries for the radio and they were on the to buy list. She'd have to pick up some the next time she was in the city. Should have done it when she'd been there for the doctor appointment, but she'd forgotten the list with everything they needed at home.

"We'll be fine," she soothed.

But her daughter was scared as her face was now beet red; her eyes were scrunched tight and tears ran like rivulets down her face.

The wind howled like a pack of wolves, scaring both of them. The basement was spooky and damp so they'd only go down there in an emergency. Instead, JJ brought them into the safest room without any windows. The bathroom on the main floor.

Despite leaving the door open for light, it was much quieter in here. She pulled the toilet seat down and sat, hugging Chrissy to her chest, pressed her mouth against her warm chubby cheeks and rained kisses upon her wet face.

The thunder kept cracking and Chrissy just kept on crying.

Then JJ joined her.

•  •  ⚓  •  •

DAN STOOD ON THE COVERED porch of the Misty Lake cabin, sipped his after-supper coffee and tucked his chin deeper into his coat to fend off the chilly ferocious wind.

He watched the rain as it poured down in thick white sheets, disappearing beneath the abundance of ferns surrounding the building. He swore he had never seen so much rain. Thankfully, the old metal roof was holding up under this crazy wind as there didn't appear to be any leaks in the rustic ceiling.

Yet.

He could tell someone had been here since his visit last autumn. Someone had left dried goods in the cupboard, so he was good for food for a few days, if it came to that. An old rope had been strung over the wood stove, most likely to dry wet clothes.

Probably Daegen and Milena from Snowy Creek Ranch earlier this spring when they'd passed through to check on their elderly neighbor, Jane, Sunflower, who ran a lamb ranch several miles from here. Or it could simply have been passerbys portaging in their canoes from one lake to another lake while interior camping. They could have seen the cabin from the lake and stayed for awhile, leaving goods for whomever came next.

Dan smiled despite the lightning sizzling overhead and the boom of thunder. He was lucky to be calling this land his home. Lucky to have such a caring woman like JJ in his life.

Tonight would have been their night together. He hoped Rafe was with her. He hadn't been able to make out her answer before the line went dead. Rafe would keep her and Chrissy safe.

He'd been in the process of burying the ripped apart carcass of a dead cow which appeared to have been taken down by wolves, when he'd heard the first rumblings of the storm. The thunder had sounded ominous and his instincts warned him to seek shelter as fast as possible. He'd made it to their Misty Lake cabin when the storm had broke. It had come on so quickly and with this nasty wind, he knew some trees would fall and block the trails.

He was glad he was here. He wouldn't want to be out in this weather. He'd have to rest up as he had no doubt there would be lots of chain sawing to do once he started back toward home.

His thoughts drew to the newbie. Ever since JJ had announced she was pregnant and they didn't know who the father might be, he'd begun thinking that he should be careful with his own life. If he was the dad, he wanted to make sure he stuck around to teach the kid fishing and hunting and all the things Brady was doing with Chrissy, like tapping maple trees in the spring to make maple syrup.

Even though she wasn't biologically his child, it was a joy to take care of her as if she were his own. He could only imagine what Brady must feel toward her, knowing she was his kid.

Dan kind of wished this baby JJ was carrying was his child. But even if it wasn't, he prayed the baby was healthy. A girl or boy, all that really mattered was a healthy baby.

A blade of lightning sizzled through the dancing trees breaking him from his thoughts. Two seconds later, thunder roared. He wasn't worried about a forest fire happening with all this lightning. Not with this downpour.

But the fierce wind was another story, especially with their routes going through some mature forests. They'd cut a good portion of trees down to make their atv trails, however there was always trees that were dying and falling over and just too many trees to cut to make larger trails. The ranch house was safe from falling trees as any potential threats had been cut down years ago when they'd made the clearing for the ranch house. And the two-story log structure with metal roof was pretty sturdy and would hold up easily in this wind. To ensure there would be no fires, they'd put lightning rods on all the buildings.

He wondered how the cattle were faring in the various pastures. Being in the open like they were in this kind of storm would surely scare the animals. But they'd most likely hunker down in the shelter of the surrounding trees beside the meadows in which the cattle were corralled. He just hoped some trees didn't fall on the cattle. It wouldn't be the first time.

Well, there wasn't anything he could do about it, so no need to worry.

He tossed the remainder of his coffee over the rustic railing and headed back inside the one room cabin. He'd go to sleep early and start out at daybreak. He just hoped the storm was over by then.

. . ⚓ . .

THE STORMY WINDS RAGED on for the rest of the day and JJ was able to get herself and her daughter calm. There was nothing she could do about the nasty storm noises, so she heated food and milk for Chrissy with pots and pans on the permanent grill in the living room fireplace hearth.

She'd built a cozy fire with the wood they kept in a large box nearby. The cheerful flames and the snapping and crackling of the fire kept them company.

While Chrissy napped in the play pen, JJ focused on feeding herself after the morning sickness went away. She also distracted herself with some dusting and reading by an oil lamp. When Chrissy was awake, she played with her.

At night, she placed the baby in the nursery crib knowing it was best to keep to their routine, despite the stormy night. Heck, if the house were to blow away, it would have done it by now, anyways.

Right?

JJ caught snippets of sleep throughout the night, waking many times to check on Chrissy. Thankfully, her daughter slept soundly. It was only when the storm broke pre-dawn and the wind died that JJ fell into a deep asleep.

She awoke with a start and gazed toward her windows. It was sunny outside. Anxiety pummelled her as it always did when she didn't get enough rest. She wished she could stay in bed, pull the covers over her head and just go back to sleep, but she had to get up. Chrissy was most likely awake or would be soon.

Groaning, she whipped aside the comforters and quickly went into the nursery. Chrissy was awake and she quietly stared up at her and JJ forgot all her woes.

"Hey, baby, we made it through the night," JJ whispered as she lifted her from the crib.

A moment later, she was thrilled to discover the power was back on and there was warm water to fill Chrissy's bath basin.

Her daughter tremendously enjoyed her baths and as usual her hands and legs splashed around as JJ bathed her. By the time JJ was finished, Chrissy was laughing and JJ was soaked.

"Oh, you are a little rascal, this morning, aren't you?" JJ shook her head and wrapped her wiggling, giggling daughter in a warm towel. A little while later, her baby was dressed in a snuggly pink knit jumpsuit complete with warm socks, dry diapers and the dreaded morning sickness was clutching at JJ's tummy.

Breakfast was quite stressful as Chrissy refused to eat and JJ had to rush to the bathroom a couple of times to vomit. There were telephone interruptions from both Rafe and Dan. They had thankfully survived the storm and they'd also wanted to talk to Chrissy. Hearing their voices only got her animated and she'd kick her legs and laugh as they spoke to her.

The guys had informed JJ that it would take a better part of a day, if not longer to clear a way home. She offered to go and pick them up at one of the lakes on the property with the float plane, but they thought it would be best to get the job done right away. Neither man had an idea if they would be back by tonight but assured her they had enough food.

Because she missed her men, she felt like crying. She hadn't heard from Brady today or yesterday and she knew in her heart if she could just hear his voice, then she would be okay.

Thankfully, Chrissy accepted a bottle of warm milk and drank it all, and had half of a second bottle, so she'd tossed the untouched food and hoisted her daughter from the chair, burped her and then hugged her.

"How about we go outside and check for damage," she said as she walked down the hallway, then pushed open the mud room door and stepped outside.

Chrissy closed her eyes as the bright morning sunshine greeted them. JJ inhaled deeply and enjoyed the mild pine scented breeze drifting in from the north. She gazed toward the lake where a white mist shrouded everything. She could barely make out the silhouette of her plane and she was grateful it was still moored at the dock. A couple of large trees had toppled at the edge of their clearing, but the barns and other buildings all appeared to be intact.

At the side of the house, she found the tipped over portable playpen nestled in the bushes where she'd seen it crash into yesterday. After checking it for damage, she was impressed it was as sturdy as ever. She placed it in the sunshine so it could dry.

Then she carried Chrissy between the rows of vegetables. The dirt pathways were relatively dry due to the strong sunshine and she assessed the tiny plants covered with an abundance of chicken wire cages that protected them from predators.

To her surprise, not one cage had blown away but some of the raised beds had been washed out. Dan had done a very good job in securing the cages, however, there was damage to many of the sprouting plants. She would dig up the ruined ones and replant as it was still early in the season.

Overall, the garden didn't appear as bad as she'd imagined it would be.

Huh, all that freaking out for nothing.

JJ frowned and shook her head. When would she learn to stop worrying about things that were out of her control?

. . ᴔ . .

MAN, MISTY LAKE SURE did live up to its name, Dan thought as he stared out across the mist cloaked lake and sipped his mid-morning cup of coffee. He had slept fitfully last night, due to the loud pounding rain upon the metal roof.

Once he'd left the cabin and had worked to clear the trail for a quarter a mile, his phone suddenly had service. He'd been in touch with Rafe, who'd slept in the tent and survived to talk about it. Rafe had also hit the trail early and both men realized there were plenty of fallen trees to clear. The plan was to cut their way through their individual trails and eventually meet up and start working together as they headed south toward the ranch.

It was brutal work, clearing the trees, but Dan figured he'd made some pretty good headway. For a break, he'd returned to the cabin for an early lunch and to get away from the mosquitoes that plagued him.

He'd planned to go right back out again after eating, but the lure of sunshine streaming through the forest and the glistening raindrops nestled on green leaves and ferns had attracted him to the woods.

At the cabin, he'd changed his sweaty clothes. Then changed his damp socks and safety boots for a fresh pair of socks and his comfortable running shoes and headed toward the lake with coffee in hand.

It was incredibly peaceful here after the constant buzzing of the chainsaw and mosquitoes. Squirrels chattered from nearby tree branches and a fresh breeze whispered against his face.

He wished JJ were here. She would love the view.

He grinned as he realized she was probably experiencing similar scenery back at the ranch house as she gazed out at their lake. But still, they should get her away from the ranch house more often. The only times she got free these days was via that float plane.

He knew she loved flying. He could see the appreciation of her surroundings shining in her eyes when she described the giant moose or black bears that strolled in the meadows while she watched from up above.

Nonetheless, he would also enjoy having her company while he worked.

He strolled closer to the shoreline. It was sandy here. They could put in a dock. This lake was big enough for the plane to land and take off. They could meet here sometimes for lunch.

Man, he really should keep his mind on all the work he still needed to do and get his mind off JJ and stop fantasizing about building docks for lunch dates.

He took another step and screamed as pain, unlike anything he had ever felt before, ripped through his right ankle. His right leg gave out and he fell over sideways.

With his left leg, he kicked blindly at whatever animal had clamped its jaws around his ankle but the slicing shards of blistering agony caused a weird light-headedness with black waves to hover at the edges of his vision.

He stopped kicking. He couldn't see any animal in the tall grass. Had it already run away?

What had just happened? Had he been shot? He hadn't heard any gunshots. What was going on? Why couldn't he move his right leg?

Shit! He didn't even have his phone on him to call for help! His heart almost crashed through his chest at that thought and then something snapped inside of him and an odd calm enveloped him.

*Just breathe. Nice and slow. No good to panic. That accomplishes nothing.*

The dark waves hovering at the edges of his vision subsided.

Fuck! His ankle and foot were killing him!

He grimaced as he tried to lift his leg. The black waves returned and he felt lightheaded again. He groaned and assessed what was going on. Through the grass he was able to see something that made his stomach lurch.

He'd stepped in an animal trap! The metal jaw was clamped around his ankle and from the rusty appearance, it must have been here for some time. All he needed to do was find the spring and set himself free. Then he could hobble back to the cabin and call Rafe for help.

His ankle throbbed with a menacing pain as he managed to reach down and touch the trap. He found there were two springs that would need to be pushed down at the same time to get himself released.

He pushed on both of them.

It didn't budge. He pushed harder. Nothing happened.

He pressed even harder, but the light-headedness swooped in and he forced himself to stop before he passed out

Oh damn. He was in big trouble.

. . ⚓ . .

JJ HAD RECEIVED ANOTHER call from Rafe later that afternoon saying he definitely would not be back tonight. She explained she hadn't heard from Dan since this morning and Rafe said he hadn't either but assured her that Dan was trained in chain sawing and probably just lost track of time.

He would try to contact Dan later and if he didn't hear from him, he would start cutting the trails toward Misty Lake. Despite his assurances that Dan was just busy, JJ couldn't shake the feeling something was terribly wrong.

It was days like these that she didn't like being here alone, but she knew she had to suck up her worry because she didn't want to live anywhere else. She kept herself distracted by entertaining Chrissy, as well as getting some cooking done. When the guys got back, they would be hungry.

For Chrissy's late afternoon nap, JJ decided to let her sleep again in the playpen. The baby went to sleep almost right away and JJ feeling pretty tired herself after a restless night decided on a nap herself. No sooner had she lain on the couch with a comfy pillow tucked under her head and she was fast asleep.

She dreamed of her cowboys. Dreamed of Brady and his sweet smile. Of Rafe and his sexy stares and of Dan's sense of humor.

Warmth enveloped her as she wondered who the father of her unborn baby might be. It could be any of her men. She'd had unprotected sex with each of them and she couldn't for the life of her remember in what order she'd had that unprotected sex with them.

It could have been with Brady that one night he'd made love to her up against the side of the ranch house after he'd lured her out to watch the falling stars. Or with Rafe when they'd had unexpected sex after working in the garden and showered together. Or with Dan that one time he'd come home early and he'd taken her from behind while she'd been removing laundry off the line.

JJ blew out a tense breath. There were other times too. Just thinking about the hot sex had her wishing for one of her cowboys to get home tonight and fast.

She loved each of the guys so much that she just didn't feel it were possible that her heart could take even more love. But it did everyday. She loved her daughter and she loved her unborn baby.

A strange little sound had JJ suddenly awake. She wasn't sure if she'd dreamed the noise or if it had been somewhere in the house. For a second, she felt disoriented and then realized she'd fallen asleep on the sofa.

She gazed over at the playpen.

Confusion rocked her as she stared. It was empty. She *had* put her baby in there and not in the crib upstairs, hadn't she?

Her mind whirled as she tried to recall and then she remembered with clear finality.

She *had* put her down to sleep right there! The blanket she'd covered her with was there but the play pen was empty.

Chrissy was gone!

# Chapter Eleven

Adrenalin and fear shot through JJ at lightning speed. Was she truly awake? Was she having a nightmare? Or had her worst nightmare just come true? Had someone kidnapped Chrissy?

Creepy crawly shivers scrambled up her back and across her shoulders as she swung her legs off the couch, sat up and frantically looked around.

Who had taken her baby? A hysterical scream started deep inside of her but she knew she would lose her mind if she didn't calm herself. She didn't scream. She did, however, try to think up possible scenarios for her missing child.

Could the baby somehow have crawled out of the playpen? How? She was too small. She couldn't even stand on her own.

"Chrissy!" she called out.

Silence.

Then she spied a piece of paper on the coffee table, right there in front of the sofa where JJ had been sleeping.

A note! Someone had left a note! Her hands shook as she grabbed it. She read it and anger tore through her.

She flew off the couch, raced down the hallway and out the mud room door. A chilly evening wind whispered against her bare arms and she shivered as she walked across the yard and gazed down toward the lake.

Standing at the far end of the dock stood her daughter's kidnapper, holding her baby. They both faced west and were watching the sun set behind the dark trees.

She didn't know why she was so angry. Her daughter was safe. Maybe she was mad at herself for falling asleep while she should have been keeping an eye on Chrissy?

Quickly she moved along the path toward the lake and forced herself to reign in her fear and rage.

Everything *was* okay, but she just couldn't wrap her thoughts around the idea that there was no danger. She decided not to tell Brady the scare she'd just experienced.

He *had* left a note. She just hadn't seen it right away. She didn't want to show him how anxious she'd become because of her scare, so she put on a bright front.

"When did you get back?" she called when she reached the dock.

He turned around and all her anger and ediginess disintegrated when Brady smiled at her.

"Hey, sweetheart. About an hour or so ago. You were dead to the world on that couch. Thought I'd let you sleep, so I took Christmas to watch the sunset. It is as beautiful as you are, baby."

She couldn't help but smile.

"Compliments will get you everywhere, cowboy," she said as she strolled past her moored bush plane.

Father and daughter looked so much alike. Their eyes were bright blue as they watched her approach. Their smiles were so sweet and beautiful. Brady looked tough and sexy, with his dark five-o'clock shadow hugging his strong chin and cheeks. He wore his black cowboy hat, red-and-black fleece hunter jacket and tight jeans as he held their daughter in his muscular arms.

Chrissy kicked her legs with excitement as JJ drew closer. He'd put a fleece hoodie on their daughter, woolly bottoms over her diaper and warm socks on her little feet.

He was such a good dad, always making sure their baby was warmly dressed.

"Come here. You're looking cold. Snuggle with us," he said and she moved in beside him.

The solid warmth of his body against hers was just what she needed. He smelled so good. Of fresh air and a hint of soap. Having him back home just made everything feel perfect now.

"God, I missed you like crazy," he said.

His eyes twinkled with heat and love as he lowered his head. The hot impact of his mouth melting over hers made a naughty need zip through her lower belly. He wrapped his free arm around her waist and squeezed her closer to him.

Suddenly he broke the kiss and laughed as he looked down. She followed his gaze and realized his cowboy hat had fallen off his head and dropped onto the dock.

"I put it on to impress you, like that first night you came here. Although back then I wore the hat trying to entice you to drink your coffee to sober you up," he said with a grin.

Pure happiness burst through her at the memories of coming here in the dead of winter, being drunk and high on anti-anxiety meds because she had issues with panic and claustrophobia and didn't want to be on a plane. She'd been so loopy she'd had the nerve to let him know that cowboy hats turned her on and so he'd put one on to get her to drink her coffee.

"That was embarrassing," JJ laughed and swooped over to pick up the hat. She promptly placed it back on his head and then nestled against him again.

"We shared our first kiss that night," he whispered.

Heat fused her body and exquisite longing shifted through her as she remembered him bringing her to his bedroom in hopes she would sleep off the booze and drugs. But she'd pulled him onto the bed right on top of her and she'd felt quite the erection pressing against her.

JJ swallowed as the hum for sex rolled through her at the memories.

"I didn't even know you. I had never been so bold before. Being drunk and on meds certainly brought out the naughtiness in me."

"Hmm, and here I thought it was my charm," he said softly.

"It was your cowboy hat," she teased.

He chuckled.

JJ knew she was going to enjoy their alone time together tonight, but first she just had to hug and kiss her daughter. Moments ago, she'd been so frightened and horrified that something bad had happened and to have her here safe and sound was absolutely wonderful.

She snuggled against her baby and kissed her cheeks, but her daughter wanted nothing of it. She turned her head away and stared at the billowing purple tinged clouds overhead.

"You've got competition," Brady said.

"It appears so," JJ whispered.

"I wouldn't be surprised if she grows up to be a brave pilot like her mom," he said and hugged her tighter.

Her? Brave? She didn't feel brave, but then she remembered her conversation yesterday with Layla. About neuroplasticity. How she could retrain her brain by imagining how she *wanted* to *feel*.

Layla had said it had helped her to get over her grief and she thought it would be helpful to JJ. But how could she retrain her brain just by imagining how she *wanted* to feel? Was that even possible? She would definitely have to look into it, especially if it had worked for her midwife.

Chrissy smiled as her dad burrowed his face against hers, but her eyes remained riveted to the purple tinged puffy white clouds. Yes, her daughter certainly did love the sky.

"My two favorite girls in the world, here by my side. I can't ask for anything more in my life," he whispered.

JJ settled against his strong body, gathering his heat into her chilled body.

She hadn't heard a sound when he'd come home. Hadn't heard the plane. Hadn't heard Brady enter and dress their baby and take her away.

Man, she really must have been tired.

Thank God, Brady was home.

Right now, that's all that mattered.

• • ∽ • •

"OUR DAUGHTER IS THE most beautiful baby in the world, don't you think?" Brady commented several hours later, as the two of them lay together in her bed.

They'd said goodnight to Chrissy a little while ago and she'd immediately fallen asleep in her crib. The entire evening she'd clung to her father like he was a life preserver. It had been obvious she'd missed him.

He'd made up for lost time by playing with her during dinner and she'd eaten everything he offered, even some more dreaded squash that Rafe had tried to feed her the other morning.

Brady had discussed that some of his siblings had been unable to make it at such short notice, talked about Tim's funeral and that he didn't think Jenna and Ginny would last long together at Jenna's ranch because in the past they'd always fought. But JJ hoped Ginny's companionship would be of comfort to Jenna.

"Yes, she is the most beautiful baby. And it's because she is a part of you and you are the handsomest man in the world."

"Compliments, my dear, will get you everywhere," he murmured, repeating what she'd said to him earlier on the dock.

She giggled as he slipped his arm beneath the comforter, under her waist and then easily pulled her close to him. She melted against his length. He felt so strong and warm.

So safe.

So male.

"I missed you like crazy, JJ. I don't ever want to be away from you again."

"I feel the same way," she admitted.

She was so glad he had come home tonight. If he hadn't, she would have lain in bed, most likely waking up many times and worrying about her cowboys. At least one of them was home safe and sound tonight.

When they'd returned from their sunset gazing, they'd found a message from Rafe on the answering machine. The downed trees were turning out to be more work than he'd thought. He'd been in contact with Dan early this morning, but nothing since. He'd said he wouldn't be able to make it to Misty Lake tonight to hook up with him.

But he'd reassured her on the machine that Dan might likely be in a dead zone area and wasn't able to use his phone. He'd said for her not to worry, but she suspected he was just saying that so she wouldn't be uneasy. She did worry when her men were not at home and she was thankful when Brady said he'd head out at first light to start clearing trees off the trail from this end.

But from the imprint of his hard cock against her thigh, he certainly didn't have trees on his mind at the moment.

He was *very* erect.

She gazed at him and his blue eyes sparkled with need as he looked at her. His breathing sounded harsh and the tip of his pink tongue peeked out from between his slightly parted lips.

Awareness buzzed through her as he placed his hot hand, calloused and wide, over her abdomen.

"This lucky little baby will be the most beautiful baby in the world too, because he or she, is a part of you," he whispered.

Her heart warmed at his words and she saw intent in his look. She trembled with excitement as he lowered his head and she closed her eyes, his mint-scented breath stroking her senses.

Gently, ever so gently, he caressed her mouth with his lips. First one corner and then the other, teasing her with things to come.

"I always ask myself, what did I do right to get a most beautiful woman like you," he said softly.

She wanted to ask him the same question, about what did *she* do so right to get a most sexy man like him. But before she could pose the question, his warm lips moved over hers with soft-heated possession, igniting sensual nerve endings and sending sparks of arousal coursing through her mouth and deep inside her vagina.

He hardened his kiss, his tongue sliding into her mouth, causing her senses to zing. His calloused hand drifted off her abdomen and then along her inner thigh, raising the hem of her nightie.

"Don't know why you wear these things," he grumbled against her mouth, referring to her nightgown.

She grinned and held her breath when his hand slid between her thighs and she then moaned her appreciation as he dipped a finger into her moist vagina, collecting cream. Then he withdrew and began to gently massage her engorged clitoris with his wet finger.

JJ felt feverish at Brady's intimate touches. Her body heating as his finger moved achingly slow over and around her sensitive bundle of nerves, sending blood pounding through her clit and shards of sensations cascading through the rest of her.

She closed her eyes, and arched against him, her body tightening as the desperate arousal deep in her vagina and around her clitoris quickly built and spread.

"Is this what you need, babe?" Brady whispered against her mouth.

"Or do you want this?" he asked and suddenly he curled his upper body, lowering his head to her left breast.

He sucked her nipple into his mouth, plumping and licking until she was so sensitive it almost hurt. He moved to her other nipple, teasing her nub with gentle scrapes of his teeth until it burned. Then he suckled her throbbing flesh between his lips, unbridling hot sensations. He moved sexily slow, alternating her breasts until both peaks were aching and nerve endings were raw and hot.

He continued his erotic assault and she writhed as Brady's finger slipped off her tender clit and he thrust two fingers into her wet vagina. Her pussy clenched around the thick inferno and she whimpered her aching need to be fully penetrated.

He kept sucking her nipples and gently pistoning his two fingers until she was twisting against him, her hips undulating, her hands desperately grabbing his muscular shoulders and holding on.

She spread her legs wider, wanting more of him inside of her. Then his mouth was leaving her breasts and he was withdrawing his fingers. He moved over her, his arms bracing himself beside her shoulders and his blue gaze caught hers.

"I love you so much," he whispered. His eyes were hooded with intent, his red mouth parting as he lowered his head.

His thick cockhead pushed against her vaginal opening, and his hot mouth seared over hers in a possessive kiss that left no doubt in her mind that she belonged to him.

His thick shaft entered and her inner muscles stretched impossibly, clenching with welcome around his hot intrusion.

He withdrew and then he began a powerful pistoning that had her moaning at the pleasure he created. He rocked against her, his cock stroking into her over and over. Deeper and deeper with every thrust.

His tongue plunged in and out of her mouth, pistoning like a mini cock. His lips bruised her mouth beautifully and his cock was a driving flesh of molten steel, claiming her.

Her body tightened and she gyrated harder, grinding herself against him and then the ecstasy unleashed. Pure pleasure tore through her like jolts of lightning, spasming into every inch of her body, shredding her mind and burning her senses.

His every powerful stroke brought more pleasure until she was flying inside her climax. Soaring within the beautiful sensations that made her want to stay here forever.

This was bliss. Perfection.

This was love.

. . ᴄᴫ⊷ . .

LIGHTNING FLICKERED overhead and Dan cursed his rotten luck. His ankle and foot were on fire and throbbed thickly with pain. Several times he'd pondered using his jackknife, cutting into his ankle and severing his foot.

But he just couldn't bring himself to do it. Not yet anyway.

Nausea clung to his stomach like a bad lover, and the stings of mosquitoes was irritating the hell out of him. A couple of times he heard something rustling through the trees behind him, but it had just turned out to be a raccoon meandering its way to the shoreline to wash whatever it'd caught for tonight's dinner.

Despite his nausea, he felt hungry. Go figure. He wondered if JJ went through this kind of hell when she had her morning sickness. Being hungry, but unable to eat cause just thinking of food made him want to puke.

Before the nausea had come, he'd even contemplated catching a couple of frogs that hopped by, but he just couldn't eat raw frogs.

He noted that the trap wrapped around his ankle was old and rusty and as hard as he pushed on those release springs, he just couldn't open the jaw. Which made him wonder how it had closed around his ankle in the first place?

A rumble of thunder made Dan curse. He wished for a flashlight. It would help keep him company if he could illuminate his dark surroundings.

Just as he was thinking that thought, lightning flickered overhead, casting a quick glow over the rusty chain that was attached to the trap clamped around his ankle. The other end of the chain had been spiked into to a boulder that was too damn big for him to move.

What kind of an idiot used traps like this anyway? Shit, how many times had Rafe or Brady or JJ reminded him to make sure he took his satellite phone everywhere including when he went off the trail to take a whiz. Just in case, they had said.

He should have listened. If he ever got out of this mess, he'd never hear the end of it. They'd have fun ragging him for screwing up. But how was he supposed to know he'd get stuck in a freaking trap? Even if he hadn't left the phone back at the cabin, if memory served him correctly, this area of the ranch was in a dead zone anyway. A bunch of very high rocky hills was north of the lake, which cut off the satellite signals.

Parts of the trap had slashed into his ankle and he'd been bleeding. Not much, but probably enough to attract wolves if they were in the area. He'd washed the blood away several times with the lake water, but every time he moved, the jagged edges of metal dug into his flesh bringing a fresh supply of blood for the mosquitoes and other predators that might be around.

He had at least one thing going for him. His tetanus shot was up to date. A lot of good that did him being stuck here.

He shivered as chills scrambled up his back. A cool damp air was wrapping itself around him and he wished for his warm sleeping bag.

What time was it anyway? He gazed at his watch and waited for the next flash of lightning.

It came. Midnight.

Great. He'd been here a little over twelve hours.

Was anyone looking for him yet? Was JJ worried? He didn't want to worry her, especially with her being pregnant. Man, he wished he could see her face. Wished she was here. Better yet, wished he was back at the ranch, nice and snug in her arms.

Frustration ripped into him.

*Oh come on! I want to go home!*

He wanted to see Chrissy. Every time he looked at that cute kid, his heart filled with happiness. She was so sweet and cheerful and she had so much of Brady in her.

"Brady! Where the fuck are you!" he shouted. His voice echoed eerily across the misty lake.

"Is anyone looking for me!" he shouted.

The frogs that had been croaking nearby along the lakeshore suddenly fell silent.

Hell, everything was quiet.

Was Brady back home yet? Was Rafe at home? Wasn't he supposed to be heading this way? They were supposed to meet up on the trails.

He felt like shouting again. Screaming his head off in the hopes that his echoes would somehow reach the ranch even though he must be at least five miles away.

If he was smart he'd make a fire to keep himself warm. He had fireproof matches in his back pocket. There were precious few sticks of driftwood and some dried branches here and there within his reach. He should have tried to collect them in the daylight, but any movement had brought such a fierce pain he'd almost blacked out.

Besides, it was too late now. Any storm would kill the fire or turn it into a raging forest fire if it got windy.

Thankfully, all he had to do was lean over and drink from the lake to stay alive. If an infection and sepsis didn't set in and kill him first, he could drink the entire lake and stay alive until they found him.

How cool was that?

It started to sprinkle raindrops. Cold and wet against his hands and face. Dan cursed his rotten luck once again.

Oh, man. He was so screwed.

. . ✿ . .

RAFE SNUGGLED INTO his toasty sleeping bag inside the pup tent and tried to hail Dan again on his phone. For a second there, he'd thought he'd heard a couple of shouts echo through the woods. But it was probably just an animal.

When he'd called the ranch earlier, JJ hadn't picked up, so he'd left a message. He doubted Dan had made it back there, so Rafe had just kept cutting his way toward Misty Lake, hoping to meet up with him.

On his way, he'd checked on the herds, making sure there was no wolf trouble. He'd found one down. A calf, torn apart. He figured it was the wolves.

Despite the wolf trouble, they'd all agreed to never harm one. So far, damage had been minimal. But they were hungry. Usually wolves stuck to tracking rabbits, deer or moose but this pack had acquired a taste for their cattle.

They might have to revisit the idea of eliminating the problem wolf pack. Killing wolves to protect their stock was legal in this province, however the idea of doing it just didn't sit right with Rafe, or the other guys.

Rafe frowned as the phone kept ringing. No answer on Dan's end.

Finally, he hung up.

Thunder boomed somewhere to the north and lightning flashed against the cloth of the tent.

Oh crap. He hoped the storm didn't come this way. And if it did, he hoped it wasn't bad like that last one, which was one of the worst he'd experienced living here. He knew the storm had felt particularly bad because he'd been in a tent. From the vicious winds and the crazy downpours, he was surprised the tent hadn't been ripped apart.

Lucky, Dan. He was likely snuggled away in bed at the Misty Lake cabin. Or maybe he'd made it back to Moose Ranch and was enjoying JJ's love.

Just thinking of JJ made him smile against his pillow. All thoughts of lucky Dan disappeared and he drifted away into hot passionate dreams of JJ.

. . ⚬ . .

JJ SLEPT FITFULLY. Every couple of hours she awoke with a start with the feeling something was wrong. She just didn't know what.

At a little after two o'clock, she left her snuggly cocoon beside Brady, who snored like the dead, and went to check on Chrissy.

Her baby slept soundly with her thumb jammed between her sweet lips so JJ quietly rearranged her blankets, making sure she was fully covered. Then she walked to one of the nursery windows and peered out. The window faced south giving her a breathtaking view of the full moon and the mirror-like lake.

Nothing moved. Not even a breeze.

Lightning flashed against the pine trees. There was a storm to the north. Maybe where the guys were. She hoped they were warm. It was nights like these, she just didn't care for. She was a damn worrywart. Why couldn't she sleep soundly like the rest of her little family?

Just in case it stormed, she closed the slightly open window. It would dampen the sounds and not wake Chrissy. Then JJ returned to her bedroom and climbed back into bed with Brady, nestling against his hot body.

He must have sensed she needed his arms around her because that's what he did. He slid one arm under her waist and brought her backside right against his strong, hard body and flung his other arm over her and nuzzled his face against her neck.

"Everything okay?" he murmured sleepily.

"Everything is fine. Go back to sleep."

Her answer was a snore.

She smiled, and suddenly everything didn't seem so bleak anymore. She slept.

# Chapter Twelve

"Been thinking on something," Brady said as he leisurely sipped on his morning coffee and flipped the pancakes that he'd insisted on making for the two of them this morning.

Chrissy had already been bathed, changed and fed and she sat on her highchair joyfully watching her dad in the kitchen.

"What's that?" JJ asked as she packed a large cooler for Brady. She didn't know how long he'd be gone, but she was including food for him, Rafe and Dan for at least two days.

"I'll tell you later, but it involves you, me, Chrissy and the plane."

JJ frowned. Was he serious? He wanted to go out joyriding in the plane when Dan and Rafe were working their asses off clearing the trails? To say she was disappointed in him was an understatement. He had never shirked ranch responsibilities before, so why now? She wasn't sure what to say, so she said nothing.

She'd been worried since waking up. Dan had never called last night and Rafe hadn't called this morning. This neuroplasticity idea of Layla's was floating around in her head too. Layla had mentioned to imagine how she wanted to feel. Well, right now she wanted to feel happy and deliriously calm. She wanted to pretend that everything was okay and yet she knew something *was* wrong. She just didn't know why she had this feeling. Was it her anxiety? Or was it instincts?

And Brady, bless him, appeared so calm and was acting as if it were any normal morning. His happy attitude was making her even more anxious.

"And the pancakes are ready, sweetheart. We'll pour our homemade maple syrup over them and they're gonna taste really good. Let's eat!" Brady called out and started piling the pancakes onto a plate.

All JJ could do was shake her head. She would have to have a serious conversation with Brady and nip his sudden tardiness in the bud. But she could do that after breakfast, because despite her uneasiness, she was hungry.

Was it stress eating? Maybe, but whatever it was, she didn't care. As long as her morning sickness stayed away she was grateful for that small miracle on an increasingly bleak day.

· · ⚓ · ·

RAFE FROWNED AS HE stood on the porch of their Misty Lake cabin. Dan wasn't inside and it didn't look like he'd slept here either because the sleeping bag was neatly opened on the bed like he'd been ready to crawl into it. The cabin was damp and chilly and the ashes in the woodstove were stone cold.

There were a couple of dishes on the table. Lunch. He could tell from the breadcrumbs and a banana peel left on his plate. Dan wasn't one to not clean up and put the dishes away.

The sat phone had been left on the table.

The atv was just outside. His two chainsaws, protective equipment including helmet and chaps plus the gas can had been left uncovered in the trailer. Dan was meticulous when it came to their equipment and he always covered things with a tarp in case of rain when not in use, even on the sunniest of days.

It appeared as if he had just walked away with plans to return but had never come back.

Uneasiness breathed through him and he suddenly thought about that weird noise he'd heard last night. At first he'd thought it had been shouts but he'd been distracted trying to call Dan on the phone and he'd pushed it off as just some animal.

Had it been Dan?

"Dan!" he shouted.

His voice echoed into the silent early morning wilderness.

No reply.

"Dan! Can you hear me? Answer me!" Rafe called out again. Still no answer.

Where the hell was he? Why was it so deathly quiet this morning anyway?

No birds chirping. No breeze. No sunshine. Just a damp, drab, cloudy day. Kind of like his mood at the moment.

Dan had cleared a good portion of the trail, but Rafe had expected Dan would have done so much more, which was another indication something might have happened. He'd been quite happy to race to the cabin and find Dan's atv parked out front. He'd figured with the two of them cutting trees on the trail heading south, they could be back home by lunch. They could see JJ and play with Chrissy.

But, if he couldn't find Dan…

He sniffed the air.

Smoke?

Alarm shot through him. Maybe there were interior campers nearby? Maybe Dan had hooked up with them and was enjoying breakfast over a campfire nearby? Or was it a possible forest fire?

Adrenalin started pumping through Rafe and he scrutinized the entire view in front of him. There were just trees and glimpses of the lake.

He stomped down the stairs and went behind the cabin. Nothing here either. Just endless trees.

*Where are you, Dan?*

Irritation snapped through him and he walked back to the front of the cabin. He should just ride the hell out of here and get to an area where he could call JJ. And tell her what? That he couldn't find Dan?

Rafe shook his head and stomped back up the stairs to the porch. Maybe Dan had left a note inside the cabin? And he just hadn't seen it? He took one last look toward the lake, then went inside.

.. ✑ ..

DAN STARED INTO THE orange flickering flames of the small fire he'd built at the edge of the sandy beach. He'd managed to prop his back against a small sapling so he could sit upright, but he was so cold. Even his nose felt icy and he couldn't stop shivering.

He was hypothermic. That's why he'd forced himself to make the little fire. He just hoped he wasn't too late in getting warmth back into his body. He'd tried to remember the stages of hypothermia, but his mind was just a jumble of confusion and he was having trouble staying awake.

Minutes earlier, he thought he'd heard Rafe shouting, but he'd been asleep, so it could have just been a dream or a hallucination from the hypothermia.

He shivered and wished for the sun to come out and dry his damp clothes because this fire wasn't doing the job in warming him. He was thankful that the storm hadn't formed last night. Just a few low rumbles of thunder and some lightning but it had rained just enough to wet his hair and his outer clothing.

He sighed and placed a couple more sticks of driftwood onto the fire and watched the gray smoke curl toward the sky.

Huh, that smoke looked pretty. It was dancing upward and curling sideways like an exotic dancer.

His eyes drifted closed again. Funny, how he couldn't feel the pain in his foot anymore. It was just a swollen throbbing mess. That's why he liked to sleep.

Sleeping made him feel peaceful. Nice and calm. Made him forget that he was probably going to die out here of exposure and his corpse would be found full of crawling maggots and flies. Oh, man, and the smell would be so bad.

"What the fuck are you doing? Why didn't you answer me?"

Dan's eyes snapped open as the questions echoed in his ears. Was he hallucinating again? Or was he talking in his sleep? Or had he been dreaming?

A branch cracked close by and uneasiness zipped through him.

Oh, oh! The freaking wolves had found him. They'd smelled his blood and were coming for him.

Dan dragged out his jackknife.

Another branch cracked, closer this time. The wolves were circling him.

He'd heard growls last night, but he'd just talk and everything would go quiet.

"Get lost, will you," he managed to say between chattering teeth.

"Dan! What are you doing? What's up with the fire?" The voice. Rafe's voice. He sounded pissed off. It was so close. Right behind him.

He had to be hallucinating. But hell, he'd take a hallucination as company anytime.

"I hope you brought along some beer, Rafe. I need to put enough alcohol in me so the maggots won't get me. Time to party, my man."

He heard Rafe curse up a storm and smiled. At least Rafe was going to keep him company. He wouldn't die alone.

Man, he was so lucky.

. . ⚓ . .

WHAT SHOULD HE DO? There was an animal trap clamped around Dan's ankle and Rafe couldn't think of what he might be able to use to remove it. He'd already tried to push on the rusty release springs, but nothing had happened. Had tried to open the jaw. But it was steadfast.

Dan looked as pale as a ghost too. Hell, worse.

A sense of urgency was sweeping through Rafe. How long could someone's foot be caught in the trap before it was compromised? It was quite swollen and red.

"The springs are rusted. Doesn't want to open and I am freaking cold" Dan muttered.

Rafe stood and looked around for more dry wood. He found some and built the fire until it was giving off some good heat. He'd take a chance on a forest fire at the moment, but he doubted the fire would catch as Dan had built it on the sandy beach and the nearby tall grass and saplings were damp.

"Okay, buddy. Just hang in there. I'm going to head back to the cabin and see if I can find something to pry open the trap. A hammer or axe might do the trick. I can pound the springs. I'll bring something warm to cover you."

Rafe knew Dan was hypothermic. Stage one for sure, probably into stage two. He was mumbling about maggots and death. His clothes and hair were wet. It had been a damp, chilly night.

"Here's my jacket and my hat," Rafe said as he quickly removed his toque and placed it on Dan's head. Then he unzipped his blue and black fleece hunter jacket and draped it over Dan's hunched quivering shoulders. He would leave Dan's clothes on. For now.

"As long as you don't take off your clothes and snuggle up against me and give me your body heat," Dan complained.

"Ha, ha," Rafe said and turned to go. He might have to do that, but first he needed to free that foot.

"Hey, bring back something hot for the cold belly?" Dan said between chattering teeth.

Rafe stopped and swore. It would take too long to cook something up for him. He just needed to hurry.

"Leave it to you to think about your stomach at a time like this man. Back in a few minutes." For a second he almost said, don't go anywhere, but figured that was a really bad joke.

"Watch your step," Dan mumbled.

His warning made Rafe take extra care in hurrying back to the cabin.

. . ⚘ . .

THE LOW PURR OF AN airplane had Dan opening his eyes and gazing skyward. He smiled.

Look at that. He was hallucinating a white float plane flying in low over the tree line and heading toward the lake.

Over here!" Rafe shouted. He was waving his arms frantically on the shoreline a few feet away.

Huh, when had Rafe come back? How long had he slept? He spied a couple of sleeping bags tucked in around him. He felt like he was wrapped in a warm cocoon. Yeah, his nose was warm now and he didn't feel so cold anymore.

Dan blinked as Rafe suddenly produced a gun and aimed it into the sky. He jerked as the loud shot stung his ears. An orange ball sailed into the air and a long trail of white followed.

It looked pretty. Like a huge orange flower with a long white stem. Dan closed his eyes again.

And slept.

. . ⚘ . .

"OH MY GOD! DO YOU SEE that?" JJ asked as orange flashed a few hundred feet to her right. It was followed by a white trail of smoke.

"It's a flare. Someone needs help," Brady answered as he looked out the window.

"I see someone on the western shoreline, about midway, waving their arms," he said.

Cold shivers spun through JJ and her heart began to pound. The area he described was very close to the Misty Lake cabin.

"Good thing you weren't pissed off at me for too long this morning. Looks like we showed up just in time," Brady muttered. A muscle clenched in his cheek as he kept looking downward.

"Well, if you had told me earlier that you were planning on coming here, and not joyriding, I wouldn't have taken so long in the shower," JJ complained. Heck, she wouldn't have even taken a shower.

She shook her head, irritation sailing through her. Brady had told her that while she'd been in the shower, he'd taken Chrissy outdoors with him in the baby sling. With her strapped to his front, he'd secured a ramp and had driven an atv onto the plane. He hadn't told her his plans until shortly before they'd left. He'd said he hadn't wanted her to feel *rushed*. He knew her so well.

"Is it Dan?" she asked as she banked the plane to her right.

The lake looked dark grey and with no wind, the water appeared glass-like. From her new angle she could see the green forest where it ended at the sandy shoreline, which was only a few hundred yards long. On each end of the sandy area, the shoreline became rocky and went all around the one-mile-long lake.

JJ held her breath as she spotted the figure. He was still waving.

"I think it's Rafe," Brady said.

"Brady, if you can make sure Chrissy is buckled in nice and tight. I'll do a flyover and set up for the descent. When you get back, keep an eye out for anything like floating logs. I'll do the same."

"Yep, I know the drill," Brady said with a nod and quickly left the cockpit.

JJ began to circle the plane so she could come in from the east end and was thankful the clouds were not low enough to obscure her view and there wasn't any mist to deal this morning.

But she noted her breathing was coming in way too fast and she forced herself to slow it down. This was too serious a situation for her to start hyperventilating and sail into another panic attack. If the guys down there were using a flare, then she needed to prepare for the worst.

She would stay calm and bring the plane down quickly and efficiently. She had no other choice.

*Imagine how you want to feel*, Layla's voice whispered in her head. Well, right now she wanted calm.

She began her timed breathing exercises, mentally counting to four in her head, holding for four and then exhaling to the count of four.

A moment later, Brady was back, seated and buckled in beside her. Worry lines were etched around the sides of his mouth as he frowned. He remained silent as he gazed out the windows looking at the water for anything that might hit the floats.

As she set up her descent, she kept searching for problems on the lake. She knew if anything were just beneath the surface, like an island or a rock, it could slice into one or both of her pontoons causing a crash or make the plane list to one side, preventing a take off. Since the lake was like a mirror this morning, reflecting the gray clouds, she wasn't able to see anything just below the surface, but it was a risk she had to take.

Her instructor had drilled it into her that a pilot always had to visually check before going down onto a lake, whether it was familiar or not and to calculate risks. Although JJ had landed on this particular lake once before without any issues, she would never assume that there wasn't a log or something else in the water that could harm her plane. She would go right down the middle of the lake like her last time here.

When she was satisfied she could make a safe landing, she lined up the plane and began her descent.

.. ⚓ ..

"MAN ARE YOU GUYS EVER a sight for sore eyes," Rafe shouted after Brady opened the plane door about twenty feet from shore and waved to Rafe.

He'd been impressed with JJ's smooth landing. She'd glided down the middle of the lake and had brought them close to Rafe without mishap. He was proud of her. She really knew her stuff.

But she'd looked nervous and hadn't said a word as she'd concentrated on flying. He knew she was worried about what had happened to cause Rafe to send up a flare, and so was he.

From the plane, he quickly assessed the situation and immediately noted Dan was slumped on the ground near the shoreline.

"Looks like something has happened to Dan," Brady called back to JJ, who was checking on Chrissy. She was still fast asleep.

JJ nodded and he swore her face got even paler.

"You get the first aid kit and I'll get the raft," Brady instructed.

He hurried to the back of the plane, located the emergency raft and returned with it to the door. He unwound the rope attached to the raft. He held onto the rope, then pulled the plug, and tossed the raft out of the plane. The raft landed onto the water and inflated quickly. It was already ready to go. Quickly, he tied the rope to the plane so the raft wouldn't drift away.

"Do you need anything?" Brady called to Rafe as he began to undress. He'd have to swim the raft over to the shore, then get Dan in and back.

"Your muscles! And hurry!"

Brady blinked as he removed his shoes and then his pants.

Muscles. Had he heard right?

"Dan's got his foot stuck in an animal trap and I can't get it open! He's hypothermic!" Rafe shouted.

*Shit.*

"Oh my God, " JJ whispered from behind him.

Adrenalin raced through him.

"Be there in a minute!" Brady shouted to Rafe.

"I've got the kit. There's antibiotic cream for wounds, tourniquet, an emergency blanket in there for him for hypothermia," she said as she held the toolbox sized orange waterproof kit.

"Good. Toss it to me once I'm in the water."

"Okay, and when he's back in the plane, I've got an emergency electric blanket. But don't warm him up too quickly out there. Keep his hands, feet, and head cold until his core warms. I saw a bolt cutter in the toolbox that came with the plane too. It might come in handy."

"Get that, would you?" he asked as he removed his jacket, shirt and undershirt.

She placed the first aid kit beside the open doorway and hurried down the aisle toward the back of the plane.

How long had Dan been out here anyways? No calls since yesterday morning, according to JJ and Rafe's call last night had said not to worry. He should have sensed something was wrong but he'd been caught up with wanting alone time with her. Guilt pummelled him and then an idea came to mind.

"Do you have bananas in the cooler?" he called back.

He saw her frowning as she moved up the aisle toward him with the bolt cutter.

"Good idea. Yes, I do. Bananas take a long time to digest and can help raise body temperature," she replied.

Brady chuckled as he hurried to the cooler.

"I guess it's a good thing you took those online first air courses," he complimented as he tore off a couple of bananas from the bunch and then returned to the door where JJ waited with the bolt cutter. He placed the bananas on top of the first aid kit and took the cutter from her.

"If you need me to come along, I can put Chrissy in the baby sling," she offered.

He noted her pale face and the furrow of concern between her eyebrows. It would probably be better if she and Chrissy did come along, especially for moral support for Dan, but that would just take more precious time.

"I'll go alone for now. I'll come back if I need you."

She nodded.

"I'll get the electric blanket ready and some soup onto the burner for him," she said.

"Sounds like a plan. Okay, I'm going to jump."

He moved to the open doorway, clad only in underwear and shivered as the chilly air breathed against his skin. Maybe he should take his clothes along? No, he needed to jump now. Time was wasting.

The water looked dark with the reflection of the cloudy sky, but thankfully he could see the sandy bottom. Maybe eight or ten feet deep. No logs or debris to cause him injury.

He blew out a tense breath and then jumped. A second later cold water sluiced over his body, shocking him so bad that he let out a string of curses.

"Fuck! That's cold!" he shouted.

He grabbed hold of the rubber raft and gently placed the bolt cutter inside.

"Okay! Throw me the first aid kit! Then the bananas! And then the rope!"

JJ disappeared for a moment. She returned to the doorway holding the first aid kit. She tossed it and he caught it easily and hoisted it into the raft.

The bananas followed and then the rope which he wrapped around his wrist. Then he began to swim toward the shore, pulling along the raft.

Moments later, his feet touched the ground and he easily pulled the raft ashore.

"Shit, you are a life saver. Don't know what I would have done, had you not shown up when you did," Rafe said as he slapped Brady's back.

Brady's gut hollowed out in a really bad way when he saw Dan.

He appeared pale and sleepy. But Rafe had covered him with sleeping bags and he'd put a toque on his head. Dan's hands were placed outside the sleeping bag and so were his feet and legs, meaning Rafe had remembered his first aid training regarding warming the core first.

When Brady spied the trap fastened around Dan's ankle and the long chain to the nearby boulder, he saw red.

He swore like he'd never sworn before in his life. Who in their right mind would set out a trap in the middle of nowhere? By the rusty look of it, it had been here for years. He remembered Daegen telling him just a few weeks ago that the elderly lady who ran the nearby lamb ranch had told him a trapper had lived in the cabin. But that was like forty or so years ago.

Who knew how many traps the guy had left behind?

"I've tried to pound the springs on each end of the trap with a hammer and then with an axe, but nothing moves them. I've poured chainsaw oil on areas as you can see, but nothing helps," Rafe said after Brady stopped cursing.

Brady forced a grin down at Dan, who gave him a wobbly smile.

"Are you okay?" Brady asked and tossed Dan a couple of bananas.

"Been better. Thanks for the food. But I'd rather have a nice hot, juicy steak or some of JJ's beef roast."

Brady chuckled. "You'll get steak and roast soon enough. If we can't spring you from the trap, I've got a bolt cutter, thanks to JJ. But the metal might be heated, so it might not get through or take too long. But we can cut the chain. Either way, you won't be staying here for long."

"Guess it's better than cutting off my foot and eating it instead of steak and roast," Dan mumbled as he peeled the banana.

Brady almost laughed but then he realized Dan was serious.

# Chapter Thirteen

Brady shivered at that thought. Having to cut off one's own foot in order to save himself had to have crossed Dan's mind being trapped here in this way. Like some of the wolves, or other animals who chewed off their paws in order to break themselves free from similar traps.

Icy chills crept through him as he envisioned Dan having to slice through the tendons and bones with his jackknife, which was laying on top of the outer sleeping bag.

"Been trying to get the jaws open too, but the springs have corroded," Rafe explained.

"How's the foot?" Brady asked Rafe. He noticed the foot was puffy and a light shade of blue. Obviously, the circulation had been compromised.

"Had to cut his pants, his ankle is so swollen."

"You own me a new pair of pants," Dan complained with a grin.

"I'll buy you a whole new wardrobe if you keep your mouth shut," Rafe snapped.

Dan chuckled.

"See how he treats me? Wrecks my stuff and then gets mad about it."

Brady couldn't help but smile. Dan's humor was coming back. Unfortunately, Rafe wasn't smiling. His expression was solemn which immediately sobered Brady.

"I've cleaned around the wounds as best as I can with some soap and water, but that trap needs to come off now. The rest of the wounds have to be treated and he needs to see a doctor," Rafe said.

Brady nodded and noticed Dan had polished off one banana and was starting to eat the second one.

"If all else fails, we can use that metal cutting saw we have back at the ranch. But let's the two of us try to get it off now," Brady replied.

He hoped it wouldn't come to using that saw as it appeared this metal looked quite thick and would take precious time to cut through. Whoever had made this trap wanted to make sure big animals didn't escape.

"Okay, let's do it," Rafe mumbled. He moved quickly to one end of the trap, and Brady moved to the other side.

"Okay. Push down on your spring and I'll push on mine with all our force at the count of three," Brady said.

Dan remained silent. He'd finished eating his second banana and Brady could tell in the way Dan was frowning and staring at the trap, the guy was worried. Hell, he was worried as well.

Movement from the plane caught his attention and he quickly gazed over that way. JJ stood in the open doorway watching them.

Brady resisted the urge to wave.

"Okay. On the count of three. One...Two...Three!" he shouted.

Brady pushed down on his spring with all his might. Rafe did the same.

Nothing happened.

*Come on! Move!*

They kept the pressure on for what seemed like endless minutes and then he swore his spring budged. Excitement rocked through him.

"Moving!" Brady shouted.

"Yup, this one too! Press harder! Get ready to pull out your foot, Dan!" Rafe ordered.

Perspiration blossomed across Brady's forehead and he pushed harder. His biceps were starting to get sore. Rafe's face was turning red.

The jaw widened and Dan groaned as he reached over and grabbed his knee.

"Get your foot out! Now!" Rafe shouted.

Dan was moving too slowly. The poor guy was too tired, but then when Brady swore he could no longer keep pressing the spring, Dan pulled his foot free and screamed and ear-splitting cry.

"Hurts like a son of a bitch!" he exclaimed and fell onto his back.

His face was ashen and Brady thought he'd passed out, but realized Dan was gritting his teeth, preventing himself from screaming again.

Brady and Rafe let go of the springs and the jaws shut.

Brady resettled the sleeping bags on Dan, wishing he could insulate him from the cold ground by moving him onto a sleeping bag, but he had more pressing matters. He opened the first aid kit, withdrew the emergency blanket and covered Dan with it, tucking it in around his neck and chest.

"Hey, buddy. I know you want to get out of here, but I'm going to take your temperature and get you some pain meds."

Brady wanted to make sure Dan's temperature wasn't too low. Because if it was, he could go into cardiac arrest or other organ failures. They needed to prepare for that if this was the case.

Dan said nothing as Brady found the thermometer. He turned it on, then pressed it against Dan's ear. A moment later, it beeped.

"Temps a bit low, but you'll live," Brady reassured.

He slipped his fingers against Dan's inner wrist to check his pulse.

"A bit fast, but not bad," he stated.

"How's he doing?" Rafe asked.

"We got to him in time. He'll live to torment us," Brady joked.

He was glad to see a smile flitter across Dan's lips.

"Can you give him some pain meds, Rafe? I'll set up the first aid so I can clean those wounds with some of those antiseptic towelettes and wrap the ankle with gauze," he nodded to the first aid kit.

"Should be a coffee mug around here somewhere too for water. Couldn't find it," Dan murmured.

For a minute Brady thought maybe the guy was hallucinating, but then Rafe was stomping around in the tall grass and he suddenly swooped over and produced a coffee mug about ten feet away.

"A hell of a way to enjoy your coffee break," Rafe chuckled.

"It literally took my breath away and I wasn't even finished the coffee," Dan complained.

"I've got bottled water for the meds," Rafe said and produced a bottle of water from a knapsack Brady hadn't noticed nearby.

As Brady removed a pair of packaged gloves, the towelettes and antibiotic cream from the first aid kit, Rafe found the pain meds, popped off the lid and placed two pills in his hand. Then he moved to Dan and assisted him into a seated position and gave him the pills with water from the lake.

"Dan, this is going to hurt but I need to wash out the wounds and get some antibiotic cream into them in hopes of preventing infection."

"Yup," came his reply as Brady positioned himself near Dan's swollen foot.

The jaw from the trap had shredded his skin and there were a couple of gaping holes where blood oozed from. All of the other areas where the jaw of the trap had clamped around were bruised blue and yellow. No sign of any broken bones protruding out of the flesh; however bones could have been broken. They would need x-rays to check.

Brady prayed it looked worse than it appeared. He got to work quickly, ignoring Dan's moans and groans as Brady cleaned the wounds as best he could. Then he applied the antibiotic cream and wrapped some gauze around the ankle. When Brady was finished Dan was cursing him up and down and Rafe was wincing and chuckling.

"I'll get the fire out, then we are out of here!" Rafe growled.

He quickly moved to the beach and began dousing the fire by cupping his hands in the lake and tossing water onto the flames. The fire hissed and sizzled in agony and white smoke billowed straight up into the air.

Brady tossed the used items into a plastic Ziplock bag that he found in the kit and then placed the bag and the kit into the raft. He grabbed the bolt cutters and as anger surged through him, he cut through the rusty chain that had held Dan and the trap hostage.

"Gonna leave the trap here for now, but I'll come back for it and do a sweep of the area with the metal detector," Brady reassured as he caught Dan's narrowed gaze focused on the animal trap.

"Let's carry him over and get him out of here," Rafe growled.

"Come on. I'm fine. I can get up on my own," Dan argued as Rafe and Brady circled him.

They ignored his protests and slipped their arms under his armpits and slowly lifted him into a standing position. It was obvious Dan couldn't put pressure on his leg. He didn't have good balance either. He was probably head rushing from them getting him up too fast.

"And I don't need no doctor," Dan complained as they hoisted him off his feet and carried him to the raft.

"You're seeing a doctor. We have to check for broken bones, blood clots, circulation issues, shit like that and see how much the foot is compromised," Rafe said firmly.

"Yeah, your foot is top priority. How the hell are we supposed to run this place without our hardest worker?" Brady said and winked at Rafe.

A bit of relief pushed through Brady as Dan chuckled.

They lifted him into the raft and Brady and Rafe went back for the sleeping bags. A moment later, they tucked Dan in nice and snug.

"Man, I cannot wait to see JJ. I hope she's gonna be my nurse," Dan said with a wink.

"She's been worried about you," Brady replied as he waited for Rafe who was undressing.

They would both go into the water and pull the raft to the plane where JJ was now waving to them.

"How is he?" she shouted.

"I'll be running marathons in no time flat!" Dan shouted back. He was grinning from ear to ear and Brady sensed he was going to be alright.

.. ᴖᴗᴖ ..

IMMENSE RELIEF SWEPT over Dan as Brady and Rafe helped Dan into the plane. Before he could even say hello to JJ, she was hugging him and smothering him with kisses.

The instant her warm arms wrapped around him; Dan knew he was going to fight like hell to make sure he was healthy. He needed to be strong for her and for the baby she was carrying. It didn't matter any more if he wasn't the biological father. He loved her and the kids, no matter what.

"I'm so glad you're okay," she whispered and finally let him go, tears were streaming down her cheeks.

"Getting so much attention. I gotta do this more often," he joked. Damned if he would ever get his foot caught in a trap again though. From here on out, he'd be watching his steps.

JJ smiled and rustled his hair.

"Once we get airborne, I'll call the doctor and see if he can't come out right away. Layla mentioned he had an Xray machine."

"A doctor who does house calls?" Dan asked.

"He's that new bush doctor. I met him. Long story. I'll tell you later. But he seems nice."

Dan brightened. Maybe he wouldn't have to go to the hospital after all? Maybe his luck was changing for the better?

Suddenly he just wanted to spend as much time as possible with JJ. Truth be told, he'd tried to avoid thinking of her when he'd been trapped because every time he did think about her, he thought he'd go nuts. He hadn't wanted to die and never see her again.

Hadn't wanted to bring her any heartache and that's what he would have caused if they'd found his maggot riddled corpse. He'd been seriously contemplating cutting off his foot. That is, until the hypothermia had kicked in. Then he'd just gotten cold and gone into survival mode, created the fire and tried to get warm. Later he'd become too confused to lop off his foot.

He spied Chrissy strapped into her special chair. She was sleeping so soundly, totally oblivious to the turmoil around her. His heart burst with love for her. To be able to see her cute chubby cheeks again was a miracle.

"Come on, let's get the clothes off and then we'll elevate that foot," Rafe said.

"Let JJ do that. She can kiss my toes and make them feel better," Dan chuckled.

But JJ was already gone.

Dan gazed down at his swollen foot and tried to wiggle his toes. Nothing moved. He wished he could feel something besides pain. Anything, to give him a bit of hope.

"Sorry man, leave your foot fetish for another time," Brady chuckled. "JJ's gonna be busy flying the plane, so you're stuck with us. I'll get all the stuff inside. We can get the rest of the gear we left on the shore when we come back," Brady replied.

*I'm never coming back here*, Dan thought as Brady moved toward the open doorway of the plane. Quite the turn of his thinking. Yesterday, he'd wanted to put a dock here and have picnics with JJ and today, he wanted nothing to do with this place. Ever.

He'd just dodged death here. There was no way he was returning to this scene to give the invisible forces another stab at taking him out.

"Just stand here and hold onto this seat for support," Rafe ordered from behind him.

Dan did as he requested and didn't protest when Rafe began undressing him. He felt exhausted and his clothes were damp, but the sleeping bags Rafe had covered him with had managed to keep him warm enough.

Rafe had saved his life. He owed him big time. And JJ and Brady had showed up just in time too. They all had saved his life.

Suddenly he felt very lucky to get out of this alive.

His gratitude deflated.

Unless he lost his foot. It didn't look good, all swollen and burning with pain. He almost preferred the numbness he'd experienced before the trap had been removed. The circulation had been compromised and he knew if circulation were stopped or hindered for long enough, the flesh died and an amputation would be necessary to save his life.

His gut hollowed out. He didn't know what he'd do if he had to have his foot lopped off. But he knew he'd deal with it if it happened. He'd have no choice but to deal with it. It was insane how things had changed within a twenty-four-hour period. Yesterday morning he'd been full of energy while chain sawing on the trails, today he could barely move.

Once Rafe had his clothes off, he helped Dan sit on a nearby warm seat. He realized it was an electric blanket heating his butt and back. It appeared to be a double size as he was able to wrap it all around him. But it was only on mild and he knew they were slowly warming him up as per medical guidelines.

He watched as Rafe dragged a crate into the aisle and placed a blanket on top.

"Here, let's get your foot elevated," Rafe said. He kneeled down and gingerly moved Dan's leg until his foot was up on that crate.

"Hey, where's my glass slipper, Prince Charming?" Dan teased.

Rafe rolled his eyes, not in the least bit amused. He frowned and moved out of his view.

Dan couldn't help but chuckle. He really should stop bugging Rafe; the guy had done so much for him, but he was just so elated to be out of that trap.

He blew out a breath as he realized his emotions were seesawing. One minute he was happy, the next instant he was worried over his foot, the next minute he was joking.

"Here's some mild soup. Drink it slow," Rafe instructed as he handed Dan a mug filled with what appeared to be broth.

"Thanks," Dan said as he accepted the mug.

"All the thanks go to JJ. She's stocked this plane with all kinds of necessities for emergencies. I would never have thought to keep an electric blanket or a burner on board. Didn't even know you could plug one in here. She's really looking out for us," Rafe said. Pride flowed through his voice and he placed a hand over Dan's shoulder and squeezed gently.

"We're really lucky to have her." Rafe whispered.

Dan nodded.

He forced himself to concentrate on sipping the mild soup as his vision blurred with tears. Emotions thick and raw threatened to bubble up from deep inside his chest and he didn't want anyone to see him cry because he was so grateful to be alive and out of that trap and now realizing JJ was stocking the plane in case of trouble...well, hell, he hadn't cried since he was a kid and he wasn't about to start now. He took several deep trembling breaths until he felt a semblance of self-control return and then he continued to sip on the soup.

As Rafe said, they were really lucky to have JJ.

She truly was their forever girl.

JJ trembled as she sat in the cockpit and prepared the plane for takeoff. She'd expected Dan to look so much worse than he did. Sure, he appeared haggard but he was talking and joking with the guys and she was so relieved she could cry. She thought she'd never have her three men together again. What would she have done had they not gotten to

Dan in time? What if he'd died from exposure? Thank God, Brady had decided he wanted to be flown in to work this morning or Rafe would have been on his own trying to help Dan.

She bit her bottom lip and prevented a gush of emotions from overwhelming her. She needed to stay focused and get all of them out of here.

A few minutes later, Brady gave the all clear. The raft had been deflated and all the items were inside, the door was shut, everyone was buckled in and they were ready to go.

"Good to have Dan back, eh," he said with a wink as he sat down beside her and buckled himself in.

"Very good. The instant I'm clear of those hills we'll have reception and I'll see if we can find that bush doctor." She'd already tried to call out, but Rafe had been right about this place being in a dead zone.

Brady nodded and JJ started the engine. She took a few precious minutes to angle the plane around and then she headed down the middle of the lake, gathering speed as she went. She listened to the water splash against the pontoons and watched the trees draw closer and closer in front of her and then relaxed when the pontoons left the water and they were airborne.

Usually she enjoyed the scenery. Loved viewing the tapestry of green forests and meadows and the ribbons of blue rivers and patches of lakes. The scenes made her feel free and happy. But not this morning.

She felt tense and worried for Dan, despite him looking better than she'd expected. She was worried about his foot. It had looked quite swollen and there was some serious bruising around his ankle.

She flew low, under the gray clouds and called Layla's number because she knew it by heart, as she'd left the bush doctor's number at the ranch. She was tremendously thrilled when Layla answered on the third ring.

JJ explained the emergency situation and her midwife said she'd contact Dr. Willie herself and would get back to JJ as soon as possible.

That Layla was willing to talk to her ex-husband when she professed they hated each other, was a good sign. Maybe the two of them would eventually get back together?

She was surprised when Layla called back almost immediately with the news the doctor would meet them at Moose Ranch within the hour. He was just finishing a house call in the general area.

She smiled over at Brady who'd been listening. He did a fist pump and yelled back to Rafe and Dan that the doctor was on the way. The guys let out a couple of loud whoops, followed by Chrissy who started to cry.

Thankfully, the ranch was now in view and she'd never felt so relieved to be home with her little family.

. . ⚓ . .

*TWO HOURS LATER...*

"No broken bones, according to the radiologist report," Dr. Willie said as he turned away from his personal laptop and faced JJ, Dan and Rafe, who held a quietly curious Chrissy in his arms.

While the doctor had stayed with Dan in the first-floor guest room, the rest of them had eagerly awaited the results from the X-rays the doctor had taken with his portable X-ray machine. JJ had busied herself by changing, feeding and playing with Chrissy.

They'd eaten some of the sandwiches she'd prepared this morning for the guys and then Brady had left to start clearing the trails from this end to stay distracted and wanted her to call him the instant they had news. Rafe had taken over babysitting duties while JJ had started working on supper for tonight.

She found it wonderful that Dr. Willie had a portable X-ray machine and had sent the X-rays through his computer to a radiologist who did emergency reviews. Ninety minutes later, the radiologist had sent his interpretation.

Relief poured through JJ that Dan didn't have any broken bones and she was so grateful the doctor had come so quickly.

"I'm glad your tetanus shot is up to date, too Dan. I'll be back in a couple of days to check those wounds," the doctor was saying.

He turned to Rafe and JJ and gave Chrissy a quick smile, before continuing.

"I've told Dan all that needs to be done. And I've left instructions for his care over there on the desk. But tonight before you go to bed, I want one of you to remove the bandages and check the wounds. I've inked a couple of red areas of concern which indicate an infection is beginning. If the redness spreads beyond the inked areas, call me. Day or night. That means the antibiotic pills I have prescribed aren't working fast enough. Then we'll have to get him on an IV drip of antibiotics which will get to the infection faster. I've left new bandages so please change them every twelve hours until I get back."

JJ's tummy hollowed out with fear that Dan might have a spreading infection.

Dr. Willie must have seen her reaction for he smiled reassuringly.

"The antibiotic pills should do the trick but I just want you all to be vigilant. He's taken two pills an hour ago. Two just to start. Then I want him taking one pill every twenty-four hours for seven days. I'm also leaving antibiotic cream for him to apply to the wounds every few hours. Instructions are on the label. The cream and pills are there on the table too."

"I can take care of checking his wounds tonight. He won't slack off if I'm doing it," Rafe volunteered.

Dan made a strangled grunt and rolled his eyes and JJ bit back a laugh.

"Any questions?" Dr. Willie asked.

"Will he lose his foot?" JJ asked. She needed to know now before her anxiety about it drove her mad. She held her breath as she awaited his answer.

Dr. Willie shook his head.

"As of now, no. That trap must have somehow been compromised as it doesn't look like the full force of the jaws had taken hold. Believe me, I've seen what damage the older type traps can do and Dan got off really lucky."

"I didn't feel lucky," Dan complained.

The doctor grinned.

Shivers raced up JJ's spine. Some guardian angels had been looking out for her cowboy and she felt so grateful.

"How long should he be off his feet, Doctor?" JJ inquired.

"As I told Dan, no weight on it for a couple of days. Crutches will come in handy after that. I'll bring a few for you to choose. They are on a rental basis."

JJ nodded. She couldn't believe they actually had a fly-in-doctor now. She should be relaxing, but she couldn't stop feeling nervous. Especially now that Brady was out there alone chain sawing trees to clear the trails. He could cut himself, or one of those widow maker trees could fall on him.

"What about blood clots, Doctor..." Rafe was saying.

*Oh, Lord, blood clots.*

# Chapter Fourteen

"Yes, the possibility exists. I've put him on mild blood thinners for that too. Those drugs are also on the table. Instructions are on the label and there is an exercise sheet for him too. He needs to do them several times a day to help prevent blood clots and prevent pneumonia."

Heavens, so many things to look out for. But she would be very vigilant. At the first sign of trouble, she'd call the doctor.

This was amazing. The doctor had been here in the room with Dan for at least a couple of hours and now she understood why it had taken him so long. He'd been prescribing drugs and giving Dan instructions and exercises.

"You're a regular pharmacy aren't you, doc?" Rafe chuckled.

The doctor grinned at Rafe.

"I keep the drugs under lock and key. But I do have a licence to carry and dispense them. Back to possible blood clots. As I told Dan, if he finds at any time he is having trouble breathing or experiencing pain like cramping and or unusual heat and swelling in other areas of the body, like his arms or legs, that could be signs of a blood clot. And they can travel to the heart and lungs and cause issues. So if you would all please be attentive and not leave him alone for long periods of time, at least the next forty-eight hours, it would be ideal. Blood clots can take weeks to clear up. I'm not saying he has any, but I'm treating him for them, due to the constriction. And as I mentioned I've also given him bed exercises to help prevent clots as the case may be."

*Oh my God! Blood clots can travel and they can take weeks to go away. And there was a chance of pneumonia.*

Queasiness rippled through JJ's tummy.

Oh darn, her morning sickness was back. She had to tune the doctor out and quickly excused herself. She made it to the bathroom just in time.

. . ⌒∽⌒ . .

"IS SHE ALRIGHT?" THE doctor asked Rafe and Dan as they listened to JJ retching in the bathroom across the hall.

"She's pregnant," Dan answered. Incredible sympathy rocked through him for JJ. He'd just experienced some of that nasty nausea himself while trapped and JJ was experiencing it almost every day. How did she do it? She was so strong.

The doctor frowned and nodded.

"I see," he said.

Interesting. Usually people were happy at pregnancy news, but not this guy. How odd.

"Well, if she needs me. Just let me know."

Dan nodded.

"So, how long have you been doing this bush doctor stuff?" Rafe suddenly asked and Dan hid a grin. Leave it up to Rafe to make sure this guy was legit. Even Chrissy was smiling and blowing bubbles with her spit at the doctor.

"How about we talk about it over a cup of coffee?" the doctor replied.

"Sure thing! I'll put us on a pot, Doc. JJ's got the finest cookies on the table for us. And sandwiches if you are hungry. She makes the best steak sandwiches. I hope you aren't one of those vegetarians. Then afterwards I can give you a hand with all your stuff out to the plane, since this one here is going to be useless for awhile."

Rafe glanced at Dan and winked.

With the doctor's back toward them as he headed to the doorway, Dan flipped Rafe his middle finger. Then suddenly, the doctor turned around and Dan managed to cover his middle finger salute by reaching into the air and stretching.

"Make sure you do those deep breaths and deep coughs, I showed you how to do. Every hour when you're awake. And those leg exercises I showed you. Those will help prevent pneumonia and blood clots," the doctor reminded Dan.

Rafe bounced Chrissy up and down in his arms, teasingly smiling and nodding at Dan behind the doctor. What a little bugger Rafe was turning out to be.

"Yes, sir. Will do. Thank you very much for coming out at such short notice."

"Just don't go stepping into any more animal traps," the doctor recommended.

He turned and followed Rafe out the door.

*Don't go stepping into any more animal traps. Ha! Ha! Ha! Ha! Ha!*

Dan shook his head and gazed down at his tattered elevated foot, resting on a pillow.

"You are one lucky sonofabitch. I thought they would get rid of you," he grumbled to his foot.

He kept staring at his ankle making sure those red areas of concern weren't spreading beyond the marker lines the doctor had drawn and listened intently. It seemed as if JJ had stopped puking. He hoped she was feeling better now. He sure was feeling better being back home.

The doctor sure was a thorough guy. Checked out everything. Twisted his ankle this way and that way. Asked him to wiggle his toes, which he couldn't. But the doctor had said once the swelling went down they would move.

Man, he'd just survived one crazy ass adventure. He hoped there wasn't another one in this lifetime.

From here on out he just wanted to live peacefully on the ranch. And make love to JJ and have kids with her. But he didn't like her having to go through morning sickness.

"Why the frown?" JJ asked as she slipped into the bedroom and quietly closed the door behind her.

"Worried about you. Feeling better?" he asked. She looked better. Color had returned to her face and she was smiling.

"Yes, actually I am. You're so sweet to think about me," she said. He felt the tension seep out of his tight shoulders. He was glad she was feeling better.

To his surprise, she came around to the other side of the bed and climbed onto the mattress beside him.

"Don't worry, I've brushed my teeth and used mouthwash," she whispered. Her brown eyes glistened with joy.

Confusion whipped through him. Then he understood why she'd said what she did when she leaned in and kissed him full on the mouth.

For a few precious seconds, everything slowed down. Having JJ's sweet mouth pressing against his lips was something he thought he'd never feel again. He could hear her breathing. Could smell her sexy scent. Felt the velvet of her arms curling around his neck as she kissed him harder.

Arousal wrapped around him like a warm blanket, making his cock harden painfully. It made him forget about the pain in his dumb foot. Made him remember how good it felt to be alive, to be with JJ again.

A growl of gratefulness sifted up from his chest.

He *was* alive. His ordeal was over. His foot was saved.

And suddenly he felt so *good.*

He reached out and curled his arms around her waist, bringing her closer to him. He trembled as her breasts flattened against his chest, groaned as her mouth scalded his lips.

Then to his distress, she broke the kiss.

"We'll continue this tonight. In the meantime, sleep until suppertime. The time will go faster."

Was she kidding?

She giggled and uncurled her arms from around his neck. Then she reached down and ran a finger featherlike across the bulge of his shaft that pushed boldly against his pajama bottoms. He gulped as his cock jerked against her fingers.

"Tonight?" he questioned.

He wasn't sure he could perform with his foot being so sore but he would do his best. His gaze drifted to her mouth as she sexily licked her lips.

Then she winked.

"No worries, I will do all the work. You just lay back and enjoy what I plan on doing to you."

His cock throbbed with need and he got her meaning loud and clear.

Oral. Woah.

"In the meantime..."

She lowered her head and kissed him once again full on the mouth. His senses went spiraling.

If she kept this up, he wouldn't be able to wait until tonight, which was still a few hours away.

An eternity.

She moved away from him, grabbed the comforter and tossed it over him.

"Are you comfortable the way you are? Do you need to lie down further? I can remove one of the pillows. Do you need to go to the bathroom? Do you need something to eat and drink?"

"I'm fine." Except for his cock. It was all hot and bothered.

And the doctor had brought a bed urinal. It was still in the plastic packaging, under a nearby blanket where he'd shoved it before the doctor had called in Rafe and JJ.

"Seriously. I want you to sleep. Supper will come soon enough. And then afterwards..."

Her voice was a breathy whisper of promises.

He watched as she climbed out of bed and began drawing the blinds at the windows. She left one window slightly open for fresh air.

"I'm so glad you are home. I love you so much," she said.

Before he could tell her he loved her too, she'd slipped out the door like an excited nymph.

Dan chuckled to himself.

Damned right he was going to sleep because if he stayed awake it would take too long to get to supper...and after.

He closed his eyes and slept.

.. ❧ ..

THE VIBRATION OF HIS phone against his waist had Brady quickly turning off his chainsaw and removing his protective ear plugs and his chainsaw gloves. His heart started hammering as he withdrew the phone from the holster.

He'd been praying like mad since leaving the ranch house that Dan was going to be okay. His mouth went dry as he said hello.

"All is good." It was JJ and relief poured through Brady.

He let out a shout of happiness and then listened as she continued. She explained everything the doctor had said.

He was grateful Dan didn't have any broken bones, but concern hit him when she mentioned the possibility of blood clots and pneumonia and the start of infections. But he'd been expecting something like that.

"I'm going to spend the night with Dan. Hope that's okay with you?" she asked. She sounded bright and cheerful.

"Of course it is. I'm sure he'll appreciate you nursing him."

JJ laughed and his heart spun with contentment. He was glad she was happy.

"That's not what's on my mind, sweetheart," she teased.

"Oh. I got it," he whispered. But was Dan up to a naughty bedroom romp tonight with JJ?

"No worries, it will be your turn soon." Her voice was full of promise and he wondered what she was up to. He bet he would find out one of these days.

"Now get back to work. But I want you back here at five sharp for supper, okay." she demanded.

"Will be there, sweetheart. Give Chrissy a kiss from me."

"I will. Be careful. Please. See you soon, baby," she replied and then the line went dead.

Brady removed his helmet and wiped sweat off his forehead. Then he gazed around at the whiplash of trees he still had to cut through. The storm had done some good damage along the main trail, but that didn't seem to matter anymore.

Dan was okay. Not out of the woods, yet. But okay.

Right now, that's all that really mattered.

. . ❧ . .

RAFE CHECKED DAN'S wounds and changed the dressings as he'd promised the doctor he would do. Everything looked good. No sign of infection spreading. He'd made sure Dan was up to speed with his meds too and emptied his urinal.

Even Dan looked good as he sat in bed, the supper tray on his lap while he devoured the roast beef, mashed potatoes and vegetables JJ had prepared for supper. Rafe kept quiet as he sat on the other side of him on the bed, his legs stretched out and his arms clamped over his chest as he watched his friend eat.

Dan could have been dead of hypothermia by now had Rafe not found him this morning. That bad thought had been popping into his head all day and it was really bugging him that someone would leave a trap on their property. That it could have been left by the captured poachers from earlier this spring had entered his mind. But they wouldn't be using old rusty traps, would they?

Nonetheless, the possibility did exist that there were more traps abandoned around their property and adjoining properties. It wasn't going to be comfortable walking around in the woods anymore.

"What's working on your mind?" Dan asked and Rafe noted he'd cleaned off the entire plate.

"I'm worried your appetite is going to leave us with no food in the house," Rafe joked.

. . ᴄᴧᴮᴐ . .

"SERIOUSLY, WHAT'S WRONG?"

Rafe exhaled and shook his head. "Probably nothing, but something's been bugging me. Something I thought I heard last night when I was trying to phone you."

Dan frowned.

"Like? What? Wolves?"

Rafe shook his head.

"Were you shouting last night? I thought I heard something, but I wasn't sure. Figured it was an animal or something."

For a minute something flashed across his friend's face and guilt pummeled Rafe. Had it been Dan shouting for help? If so, Rafe could have gotten to him much sooner.

Dan suddenly chuckled and shook his head.

"No, I was too busy fighting off the mosquitoes," he said and then casually slurped some of his coffee

Relief poured through Rafe. So, it must have been some animal, just like he'd thought. If it had been Dan, he wouldn't have been able to forgive himself for not getting out of his tent and shouting back.

He watched Dan pick up his fork and chop off a giant piece of frosted chocolate cake and shoved it into his mouth.

He made some mighty fine appreciative sounds that had Rafe wondering what delights JJ had put into that cake. He'd delayed dessert so he could keep Dan company while he ate his supper.

He'd go grab some dessert, but he just wanted to stay here a little while longer with Dan. It was nice having the guy back here safe and sound.

"Why do you keep staring at me?" Dan asked as he shoved another forkful of cake into his mouth.

Rafe said nothing and just smiled.

Dan rolled his eyes. He kept eating and making those funny sounds.

When he finished his cake and his coffee, he suddenly got a weird smile and Rafe suspected he was up to something.

He was right.

Dan nodded toward his elevated bare swollen foot.

"Hey, Prince Charming. I'm still waiting for my glass slipper, oomph—"

Before Dan could finish his sentence Rafe smacked Dan in the head with a pillow and heard the dishes go cluttering and Dan cursing. Then Rafe flew off the bed and raced for the exit. He slammed the door shut behind him and started laughing when he heard the pillow hit the other side.

Then all was silent. Mission accomplished.

Rafe chuckled as he walked toward the kitchen. He was going to get himself a big slice of that chocolate cake and a hot cup of coffee too. Then he and Brady were taking Chrissy to watch the sunset and JJ would be keeping Dan company this evening.

Suddenly he wished he were in Dan's shoes tonight. He was one lucky guy, minus that bad foot of course.

JJ peeked down the staircase making sure Brady, Rafe and Chrissy were gone. A few minutes ago, she'd heard the slam of the mudroom door signalling they had left. She would've loved to have watched the sunset on the dock with them tonight, but she had more pressing matters on her agenda.

All of them had to do with Dan.

Brady had gone in earlier to remove the supper dishes, supply Dan with toothbrush and toothpaste and Dan had insisted he'd do his own sponge bath. So Brady had given him a basin with warm water, soap and washcloth and towels. He'd left Dan in privacy for a bit and then returned with clean water so he could rinse.

Brady had reassured her that the sponge bath appeared to have refreshed Dan and he was wide awake and seemingly bored when Brady left him. Before that Rafe had stayed with him during supper and had come out laughing. But he hadn't shared any details. She was just glad everyone was safe at home tonight.

She'd had a nice hot shower while the guys cleaned up and babysat Chrissy. Then she'd dried and brushed her hair until her brown curls shone like jewels and felt like silk. She'd slipped into one of her sexiest black nightgowns and even put on some makeup, which she rarely did.

But she looked really nice, she had to admit. She felt so special tonight. Bold and beautiful. Grateful that her injured cowboy was sheltered and tucked away in bed.

She smiled and tiptoed down the stairs, past the kitchen and into the hallway. She stopped in front of the guest bedroom door and waited.

Silence.

Quietly she opened the door. The lights were on, a cozy fire crackled in the stone hearth and Dan lay in bed. Perched on his head was a brown cowboy hat and that hat was enough to turn her on big time. She loved a man in a cowboy hat.

His well-muscled arms were crossed over his bare chest, and the brim of the cowboy hat wasn't pulled down low enough to cover his eyes and she noticed they were closed!

Oh no! Had he forgotten she was coming and fallen asleep?

She stood there for a few minutes, just watching him. The blankets covered him from waist down except for his injured foot and leg, which had been propped up on pillows. He was in a half-seated position and his back and head leaned against several pillows. His chest rose and fell slowly and he had the cutest smile on his lips. Lips she'd wanted so desperately to kiss tonight. She'd missed him terribly and hadn't realized how much until they'd brought him home.

Well, if he was sleeping, she'd just silently lay down beside him. She shouldn't have been surprised finding him asleep. After his ordeal, he needed his rest. She would only be selfish if she woke him.

She entered the bedroom and gently closed the door behind her.

She stood there for another few minutes admiring the blue-and-white gingham curtains adorning the three windows, the pine bed, and the rustic dresser.

This bedroom had once belonged to Brady, until he'd decided to move into another room upstairs. So she'd have easier access to him, he'd joked. After that, they'd brought a desk, a computer and printer in here too, now using it as a second office and guest bedroom.

To think that a woman had given birth to twins in this room just a few days ago was strange. There had been that awful storm, and then Dan's accident. Her pregnancy news before that, Tim's sudden death and her awful panic attack while flying the plane back from dropping off Brady and Mitch at the airport.

So much had happened in such a short period of time. Life had just gotten too hectic. No wonder her head was spinning. No wonder she wanted to regain a sense of control and just do something naughty for Dan.

JJ sucked on her bottom lip and slowly tiptoed around to the other side of the bed. Gently she lifted the covers on her side and quietly slipped in, laying down, but not too close to him as she didn't want to wake him.

"Was wondering when you were going to join me," Dan said softly.

His forest-green colored eyes were open and he was looking at her, that cute smile still on his lips.

"Oh my gosh! How are you feeling? How is your foot? I thought you were asleep?" She laughed.

"Feeling good, sweetness. Foot is better. And nah, was just resting my eyes. And I'm glad I did. You look really hot!"

"I'm glad you noticed," she teased.

"Woman, there isn't anything I don't notice about you," he purred.

He reached out and she curled against him, his arm beneath her waist. She loved that he had the strength to pull her close against his hard length.

"What *do* you notice about me?" she asked, wanting to know.

"Like, you are the most beautiful woman I've ever seen."

"And?"

"The kindest. The most gentle and thoughtful, sweetest..."

He stopped when she feigned a snore.

Dan chuckled.

"You're quite playful tonight, aren't you?" He hugged her even closer.

"I'm just very happy you are okay," she admitted. "And I want to show you exactly how happy, because for awhile there I thought I'd never be able to do this..."

She slipped her hand beneath the covers and felt the heat wafting off his body. She also discovered he wasn't wearing any pyjama bottoms.

Instead, he wore a very hard erection.

"I was going to ask if you were up for it, but I can see you are," she whispered.

Dan chuckled and lowered his head and kissed her. His lips moved sensually over hers, parting them and his tongue slipped into her mouth to brand her tongue.

She wrapped her hand around his velvety shaft and held him gently. She could feel his hot flesh jerk against her palm and her body ached to climb on top of him. To slide his thick shaft deep into her vagina and just ride him. But she didn't dare. Didn't want to hurt his foot.

She would put her needs aside for tonight and pleasure her cowboy. She broke the kiss.

Dan was breathing harshly as she broke the sensual kiss and squeezed his erection. Her pretty brown eyes twinkled with excitement as she repositioned herself a little further away from him.

He breathed in her scent. She smelled like flowers, fresh air and happiness. And boy, she looked so nice tonight with her tangled hair and blushed cheeks, it was almost worth being injured just to have her intimate attention.

When he'd first heard her enter the bedroom, he'd been deep in thought about lying to Rafe that he hadn't shouted last night. So, Rafe had heard him. Had Dan kept shouting like he'd wanted to; Rafe might have come sooner. But he didn't want Rafe to feel guilty, so he'd lied. He was glad he didn't tell him the truth, because he knew Rafe would have felt real bad. He didn't want that for his friend. The look of relief on Rafe's face made Dan realize he'd made the right choice with his answer.

JJ's long curly hair tickled his chest, bringing him back to the present. He blew out a tense breath as she lowered her head over his chest and slurped his left nipple into her hot little mouth. Her lips were like scorching brands as she sucked, making him gasp at the erotic sensations scrambling through him. At the same time, she stroked his cock, her velvety fingers like naughty little flames. He could feel her every touch, every subtle scratch of her fingernails. Could feel his shaft thickening, his balls tightening.

"You like this? she whispered.

He wanted to answer her, but he couldn't speak if his life depended on it. Every muscle in his body was tense, His senses on high alert.

Her hot lips moved to his other nipple and he clenched his teeth as she suckled, unleashing a foray of pleasure pain with her mouth and her teeth. Then her tongue laved at the tingling hurts. His mouth went dry as she let go of his sensitized nipple and she moved her head lower.

Her blistering lips kissed his chest, her lashing tongue crisscrossed his abdomen like little wet whips until his penis throbbed and his scrotum grew tremendously heavy.

As she angled her sexy mouth and seductive tongue toward the apex of his thighs, he cursed his bum foot for being too painful to move. But he had no trouble widening his other leg so she could have easier access.

He swore softly as she whisked away the rest of the covers. His shaft was in full erection mode, flushed red with need and aching for her mouth to wrap around his feverish flesh.

Tension intermingled with anticipation as her head dipped between his legs.

# Chapter Fifteen

JJ's hot breath caressed his penis and scrotum.

Her fingers from one hand clamped around the base of his cock, and nimble fingers from her other hand were smoothing along his trembling inner thighs. Up and down, back and forth, while her long hair tickled and tormented areas her fingers left untouched.

She opened her mouth and he jerked as her warm lips stretched around his straining cockhead. He watched as part of his cock slowly filled her mouth and he moaned as she licked underneath his quaking flesh, her hot tongue unleashing a volley of quivering sensations.

He slammed his head back against the pillows, sending his cowboy hat flying off his head.

"Oh man, you're killing me here," he hissed.

She smiled around his cock, tightened her lips and then she began to bob her head.

In and out of her mouth went his cock. The suctioning of her lips and rasping of her teeth against his rigid flesh had him clenching his fists as arousal spiraled along his pulsing length.

His entire body stiffened with need.

Instinctively he reached out with both his hands, tangling his fingers into her velvety hair, holding her head steady while she made love to his penis with her succulent lips.

His cock throbbed painfully and his balls felt like they were about to detonate. Desperate need for release made him move her head faster, and faster.

The sensations tangled around his penis, grabbed hold and squeezed. He forced back a shout.

"I'm coming," he growled his warning between clenched teeth.

But she just kept slurping and bobbing her pretty head, seemingly oblivious that he was about to orgasm. He held on as long as he could until the quavering spasms burst.

With lightning speed extreme pleasure rushed through his erection, slamming upside his balls and lancing his lower belly like a monstrous explosion. His body jerked and his thighs shuddered as he shot his cream into her mouth.

She sucked on him like a pro, doing everything right as he trembled, moaned, and twitched.

She drew on him until he was perspiring and his cock was dry and limp. And she didn't even get any of his release on him!

Then she let him go.

Her lips were ruby red and her brown eyes glittered with excitement. She beamed as with the back of her hand she wiped away his semen from her lips.

"Was that as good for you as it was for me?" she asked. Her hot expression whispered over him like a ribbons of silk and he could barely breathe.

"That was fantastic," he whispered and lay back against the pillows, totally spent.

"Back in a few minutes," she said softly. She climbed out of bed, leaving him feeling satisfied as sin, woefully abandoned and useless. He wished he could reciprocate, and bring pleasure to her, but he was exhausted and he sensed she knew it.

She'd taken a quick visit to the bathroom and then when she returned, her breath smelled all minty and fresh as she snuggled in his arms. She was soft and warm against him and he loved the lazy way she was tracing her finger around his belly button.

"They're coming back," JJ said and he heard the stomping of boots on the stairs to the mudroom.

He pulled her tighter into his embrace and they fell silent as they listened.

Rafe and Brady were talking in low murmurs and he suspected Chrissy must have fallen asleep. A few minutes later, he heard them go upstairs.

"You are an angel coming to my rescue tonight. I didn't want to spend another night alone without you," he confessed.

"I feel the same way about you," she replied.

"I've really missed being home with you," he admitted. "That damned storm brought us a bad omen, didn't it? Lots of work clearing the trails and then that stupid trap. How did you hold up in the storm anyway? Rafe said he was in the tent and Brady told me he didn't come home until the day after."

She shivered against him and that's when he knew she'd been afraid.

"I wasn't going to say anything, but Chrissy and I were pretty scared. The roar of the wind and the way the rain came down in such a torrent, I thought we'd die for sure. The power went out and neither of the generators came on like they usually do. Someone must have taken them off standby. There was no way I was going out in that storm to the shed to turn on a generator. I had awful ideas of something bad happening to me and Chrissy being here on her own" she said in a rush.

His gut clenched at the thought of her being in the house without lights or power and her horrible thoughts about Chrissy being alone.

"You were smart not to go out. Too dangerous. We'll have to make sure it stays on standby. I'll talk to the guys about it."

She nodded and pressed her hot cheek against his chest.

"I put the fireplace in the living room to good use though. I warmed up food for Chrissy and myself with pots on the grill. We were like pioneers for half a day and a night. We survived without the roof blowing off."

He knew she had one hell of an active imagination and her anxiety must have been skyrocketing the past few days, but he needed to reassure her of one thing.

"The house is safe, JJ. The windows are top of the line and can stand a lot of wind. The roof is very strong. It's got hurricane braces and built to last for centuries. The only thing that could take this place out is a big tornado or a category five hurricane. Chances are so slim of either happening; you shouldn't even think about it. There are lightning rods on all the important buildings, house included. So no fires from lightning strikes. Next time there is a bad storm and you're alone just remember what I told you, okay? You're safe here."

"Okay, I will. Thanks."

Her answer sounded confident so hopefully she'd put the storm fear aside.

"Other than that, how are you feeling? How is the newbie?"

A sweet smile whispered back to her lips.

"Our newbie is doing just fine. He or she has been pretty quiet, except for a few little fluttery feelings just to let me know he or she is there. Oh! And did Rafe or Brady tell you? Layla was here a couple of times and twins were born right in this room."

Dan frowned. What was she talking about?

"No, they didn't say anything about that," he admitted. The guys had been busy talking about ranch business with him.

He listened as she told him about the emergency. About Layla flying in with a young woman in labor. The woman's husband showing up with the doctor and the doctor doing a C-section to deliver the twins. And an air ambulance helicopter had come and done an emergency evacuation. That JJ already had her first midwife appointment and she was taking prenatal vitamins.

Wow. All the stuff she had gone through and here she was pleasuring him.

When she fell silent, he hugged her even closer. She was one hell of an amazing woman.

He sighed and felt content for the first time since getting his foot caught in that trap.

She didn't say anymore and he noticed her finger had stopped twirling around his belly button and lay limp.

He gazed down at her. Her eyes were closed and she was breathing slowly.

She'd fallen asleep.

She looked so peaceful in slumber and he dared not move a muscle. But it gave him a chance to send up a volley of prayers to the big guy upstairs, thanking him for a miracle in sending Rafe, Brady and JJ to rescue him and for sending JJ to Moose Ranch in the first place to take care of all of them.

Man, he *truly* was one blessed man.

. . ༄ . .

JJ SLEPT AS IF THERE was no tomorrow.

She had no worries. Just blessed oblivion and she found it hard to wake up. She awoke in layers. Sounds came first.

Sounds of someone breathing nearby. Soft voices of Brady and Rafe. Happy giggles from her daughter.

Smells came next. Fresh aroma of coffee percolating. Bacon. French toast.

Then all was quiet and she drifted off to sleep again.

It was so nice to finally be able to sleep without worries. No more thinking about Dan being missing. No more worrying that Chrissy would be alone if something happened to her.

But there were glimpses of wondering. About the man in the motorboat who'd come to her rescue with ginger ale and crackers. Who might he be? And there were thoughts about Tita and her family. She hoped she was well and that her husband would stay with her at their homestead instead of leaving her alone again.

She felt calm in her slumber. Even thinking about poor Jenna losing Tim in such a quick way, didn't wake her up in a panic because she could feel Dan's arms holding her. He made her feel so safe.

Suddenly she could feel the bed moving. Or was it her moving? Oh, she hoped she didn't have the morning sickness again. She forced herself not to wake up. Instead, she just went with the swaying feeling. As long as Dan's arms were holding her she would be alright.

After awhile, she wondered if maybe Dan was getting out of bed?

No! He wasn't supposed to use his foot. She had to wake up and admonish him.

JJ awoke up with a start and blinked as the bedroom rolled into focus.

Confusion rocked her. She wasn't in the guest bedroom anymore. She was upstairs. In the room with the king-sized bed. The room were the four of them spent their naughty nights.

How had she gotten here?

"Hey, sleepy head," Brady's voice drifted through those cobweb layers of after-sleep and she gazed toward the foot of the bed to find Rafe and Brady standing there.

Brady wore his black cowboy hat. And Rafe wore his beige cowboy hat.

Have mercy! The two men were completely naked!

She creamed as excitement rocked through her.

Oh, wow. Was she having an erotic dream? If so, then she didn't want to wake up.

They were watching her, massaging their long, thick erections. Lust shone in their eyes, and she trembled with awareness.

"We've decided you need the morning off. In bed. With the two of us," Rafe said in a thick voice.

JJ giggled with excitement. She wasn't dreaming? This was for real?

"Not quite the reaction we were hoping for," Brady said with a frown, but she read the teasing in his blue eyes.

"Where's—" She wanted to know where their daughter was, but Rafe cut her off.

"Dan is keeping an eye on Chrissy. We bathed, changed and fed her. Dan's taken care of too. We propped him up on the couch in the living room, and she's right beside him in the playpen with her dancing mobile and stuffed animals. He's under strict orders not to get up or pick her up unless he remains seated. He'll holler if he needs us," Rafe explained.

Concern for Dan whipped through her.

"But the doctor said we need to keep an eye on him for forty-eight hours." There was no way she was going to put Dan's life in jeopardy for her own pleasure.

"Hey, don't worry. Dan is fine," Brady reassured. He nodded to the baby monitor on the night table.

"I just turned it on. They're probably already napping as it's quiet. We can hear everything down there but they can't hear us. We'll be taking turns going down to check on them. We got this. No worries, okay?" Rafe added.

JJ nibbled on her bottom lip.

Wow, the guys had thought of everything. How could she disappoint them by not going through with their naughty idea? How could she disappoint herself? Who was she to turn down a morning in bed with two of her sexy cowboys? She'd have to be crazy.

Rafe's brown eyes darkened with heat. They were so dark they were almost black and the intensity of his expression made her pussy quiver.

"Okay," she whispered.

"Good. Just remember our baby is safe so we can take care of your naughty needs," Brady replied with a grin. His face appeared flushed with excitement and his fingers gingerly stroked the length of his shaft.

Fiery heat at his words and the demanding shade of purple showing visibly on his cock and balls made her quake with awareness as she imagined both men having sex with her.

"Dan told us what you did to him, last night. And that he wasn't able to give back. So, we're here to return the favor," Brady said.

*Return the favor.*

Sweet heavens! Her cheeks suddenly warmed.

It felt like an eternity since she'd had more than one of her men in bed with her and she wanted these two hotties to make love to her. Orally, vaginally and anally!

Going down on Dan had been awesome. She'd enjoyed pleasuring her cowboy and had adored the throb of his flesh as it had grown so solid in her mouth. It made her feel powerful knowing she could create such pleasure just with her lips, tongue and teeth.

Oral was such an intimate act. So different than anal and vaginal penetration. Oral, to her, felt so unselfish. And now Rafe and Brady were going to go down on her. Just thinking about what was about to come made her breathing grow faster and rougher.

Without warning, Rafe reached out and grabbed the end of the bed covers. With one quick yank, they were off her and she was exposed wearing only her sexy black nightie that she had worn for Dan last night.

The mattress moved as Brady climbed onto the foot of the bed. Sexual hunger tensed his body, showing off bunched muscles all over him and she could see the heavy length of his cock stabbing downward from the apex of his thighs.

Automatically she lifted her knees and widened them, eager for him to begin pleasuring her.

She whimpered as he positioned himself between her thighs and then he lifted her nightie.

"No panties. Just the way I like it," he whispered.

He looked up at her and his blue gaze sparkled with appreciation. JJ jerked as his fingers spread her folds. His fingers felt like seductive flames as he touched her there and she cried out as a digit penetrated her wet vagina. He dipped inside of her, gathered her juices, then withdrew, coating her throbbing clitoris with her cream.

Then he was rubbing and massaging. Circling and pinching. She bit her bottom lip to prevent from crying out as tension and awareness quickly mounted throughout her.

She was barely aware of Rafe, who was now sitting on the bed beside her. His scorching hands were on her shoulders as he unsnapped the straps of her nightie and lowered the garment until her breasts were exposed to him.

"Beautiful, so beautiful," he murmured.

He licked his red lips and then his head was lowering toward her breasts and JJ gasped as he palmed her mounds and brought them closer together. Then he covered the tip of her left breast, branding her with his hot mouth.

His teeth firmly gripped her nipple and he pulled. She inhaled sharply at the erotic tug that arrowed electric pleasure down to her tender clit where Brady continued to rub and massage.

Rafe tending to her nipple and Brady stroking her clit unleashed her pent-up naughty desires. Her pussy was on fire and she whimpered and jerked her hips as she craved more stimulation.

She cried out as Brady's tongue slipped past the folds of her labia and entered her vagina. His strong, moist tongue dabbed and pushed against her quivering muscles.

She gasped as Rafe's lips suckled her nipples until they were raw, rigid and on fire.

Brady's mouth then fused over her engorged clit and she cried out as both men suckled at her intimate parts igniting brutal pleasure pain that had her entire body tensing until every muscle was tight and every nerve ending was zinging.

She groaned her frustration when cool air whispered against her pussy as Brady pulled away. His hands slipped under her ass and she felt him push a pillow beneath her hips, bringing her ass up higher.

A moment later, the entrance of her anus was pushed open as a warm smooth item, the size of a large cock, entered her. Brady slowly sank the dildo into her and her ass eagerly clenched the toy.

She knew it was the self-lubricating dildo that one of the guys had bought awhile back. All Brady had to do was push the plunger and the dildo unleashed the lube inside her and that's what he was doing now, as she could feel the warm cream caress her tense internal muscles.

Then Brady slowly withdrew the toy from her clenching ass and pushed it in again. He began a sensually slow thrust and she could hear the slurp of lube echoing through the air with his every lunge. Needy sensations flowed through her. She arched her hips against the pillow beneath her and slapped her hands upon Rafe's hot back.

"That's it. Take it all the way in, sweetheart," Brady cooed as he sank the toy deeper and deep with every plunge.

While Brady made love to her ass with the dildo, Rafe made love to her nipples. Sucking, pinching and biting, searing her breasts with red hot pleasure.

JJ was shuddering now. Heated desire pummeled her every pore. She could feel the tension building. The pleasure increasing with every second.

She moaned her frustration as Rafe moved his head away, leaving her nipples erect and on fire.

Then Brady was also leaving her.

She opened her eyes and caught Brady nodding to Rafe and she sensed some secret signal zipping between them. Then Brady was walking to the other side of the bed and he climbed onto the mattress.

"On your side, baby, facing Brady," Rafe instructed. She did as he told her and rolled onto her side, coming face to face with Brady as he'd already stretched himself out beside her.

"Hey sweetie, I need you," Brady whispered, his face flushed. His breath smelled minty and she wondered how he'd managed to freshen his breath without her noticing.

JJ trembled and her pussy clenched as she gazed down and became mesmerized at Brady stroking the length of his ultra thick cock. She could see the precum glistening from the tiny slit in his large cock head. Noticed the muscles in his shaft jerking with need.

"I need you too," Rafe said from behind her. She heard the rip of plastic and a moment later she knew he was sheathing a condom.

She inhaled deeply as she felt the hot swell of Rafe's penis press against the tight knot of her sphincter. She hissed as he pushed inside, the pressure unbelievable but she loved his thick intrusion. She pushed her hips backward, allowing for a deeper, fuller penetration.

Brady stared at her as he moved closer.

"I love you so much, baby mama. Don't you ever forget it," he whispered.

JJ sucked in a hot breath as Rafe's arm slid under her waist and his other hand smoothed over her other side.

Then Rafe rolled them with her ass impaled. Suddenly she was on top of Rafe, facing the ceiling. She shuddered from the pleasure pain making her anal muscles clench around his cock.

Brady was moving over her and on top of her. His engorged penis thrusting downward as he aimed it between her thighs. Her ass throbbed, bursting with Rafe's solid velvety flesh and she cried out as the flaming need inside her vagina was filled by Brady's deep thrust into her.

She lifted her legs and wrapped them around Brady's hips, allowing for a deeper penetration.

Rafe groaned beneath her as Brady began to piston into her. Brady's tongue plunged into her mouth, thrusting in unison with his pistoning cock.

Pleasure soared through her ass and pussy with his every thrust.

He pumped hard and fast. The pleasure was spreading, and JJ shuddered as the spasms gripped her. Rafe's shaft buried inside her ass created such a heavy pressure and it made everything feel more intense.

Blood thundered through her ears as Brady kept pistoning. She felt Rafe's cock jerk and thicken inside her with Brady's every thrust.

Then she could feel it coming. A destructive explosion. She knew it was going to be a big one. A good one.

Brady kissed her harder. And JJ was shattering.

Her climax detonated. Pleasure slashed through her at lightning speed, and she jerked and moaned as spasms lashed her.

Her pussy and her ass convulsed in unison and she was thrown into a wonderful world of searing explosions and brilliant colours. The tremors rocked her and she writhed between the hard, hot bodies of the two men.

Pleasure made love to her. It was beautiful. Too beautiful.

She was barely aware when Brady ripped his mouth away and cried out his own release, his entire body convulsing on top of her.

Soon Rafe's release followed.

JJ stayed within the pleasure as long as she could because her cowboys were claiming her and she was claiming her cowboys!

The End

# More Cowboys!

Cowboys for Christmas

Cowboys Online 1 ~ Moose Ranch

Jennifer Jane (JJ) Watson has spent the past ten Christmases in a maximum-security prison.

The last thing she expects is to get early parole, along with a job on a remote Canadian cattle ranch serving Christmas holiday dinners to three of the sexiest cowboys she's ever met!

Rafe, Brady and Dan thought they were getting a couple of male ex-cons to help out around their secluded ranch, but instead they get an attractive and very appealing female.

In the snowbound wilds of Northern Ontario, female companionship is rare.

It's a good thing the three men like to share...

They're dominating, sexy-as-sin and they fill JJ with the hottest ménage fantasies she's ever had. Suddenly she's craving cowboys for Christmas and wishing for something she knows she can never have...a happily ever after.

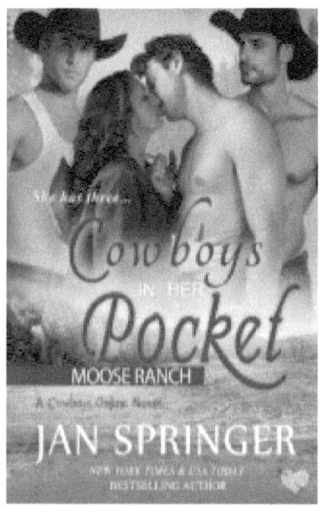

Cowboys In Her Pocket
Cowboys Online 2 ~ Moose Ranch
Jan Springer

*After spending ten years in a maximum-security prison Jennifer Jane (JJ) Watson got early parole and a job on a remote Canadian cattle ranch playing housekeeper to three of the sexiest cowboys she's ever met...*

Spring has finally arrived at Moose Ranch, and a single woman fresh out of prison shouldn't be experiencing scorching ménages with her three sexy-as-sin cowboys. But JJ's love for her men continues to grow as she gives into the fevered heat and scorching passions; she feels for each of them.

Life is perfect.

Until her new life is tested when mysterious happenings occur on the ranch and then one of her cowboys is viciously attacked and injured.

Will JJ's newfound freedom and happiness be ripped away?

*Rafe, Brady and Dan never expected to find an attractive and very appealing female to help them out at their secluded ranch. But in the wilds of Northern Ontario, female companionship is rare. It's a good thing the three men like to share...*

Brady, Dan and Rafe have never been happier. Their cattle ranch is flourishing and their continued desire to share the sexy woman who cares for them makes their life complete. Until danger threatens to rip everything apart...

Loving Her Cowboys
Cowboys Online 3 ~ Moose Ranch
Jan Springer

*AFTER SPENDING TEN years in a maximum-security prison Jennifer Jane (JJ) Watson got early parole and a job on a remote Canadian cattle ranch playing housekeeper to three of the sexiest cowboys she's ever met...*

Her love for her cowboys continues to grow as she gives into fevered heat. But JJ's simmering restlessness explodes and she's seriously making up for lost time by pursuing her dreams. There's only one little problem. She hasn't revealed to her bosses what she's been up to while they're away tending to the cattle. She knows when they discover her secret, there will be hell to pay.

Ranchers Rafe, Dan and Brady have found the woman who completes them. She makes their secluded ranch a home-sweet-home. She's vulnerable, sweet and willing to share her bed with all three of them. But when JJ's secret is unwittingly revealed, they're stunned and angry. They figure it's time to dole out some fiery punishment in some mighty naughty ways...

• • ∽∾ • •

Cowboys In Her Heart
Cowboys Online 4 ~ Moose Ranch
Jan Springer

*AFTER SPENDING TEN years in a maximum-security prison, JJ gets unexpected parole and a job on a Canadian ranch serving up scrumptious dinners and lots of hot love to three of the sexiest cowboys she's ever met.*

Jennifer Jane "JJ" Watson has never been happier. She's going to have a baby!

Thankfully their wilderness ranch is a nice distraction for her three sexy cowboys while she's away flying her plane. But when she's home, her dominant hunks are tending to her naughty pregnant cravings and that includes plenty of sizzling ménages.

Rafe, Brady and Dan don't much like the idea of their woman flying the Canadian skies and being at the mercy of the unpredictable Northern Ontario weather. They would prefer having her warming their beds twenty-four seven. But she has a way of getting what she wants and right now she needs her new-found freedom.

Worst fears are realized when JJ, her friend and JJ's plane suddenly go missing and she doesn't come back home to them.

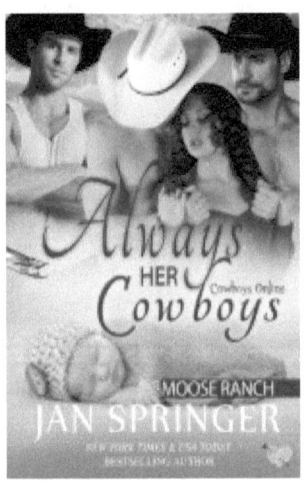

Always Her Cowboys

Cowboys Online 5 ~ Moose Ranch

A Canadian Contemporary Ménage Romance m/f/m/m

*JENNIFER JANE (JJ) Watson has spent ten Christmases in a maximum-security prison. The last thing she expects is to get early parole, along with a job on a remote Canadian cattle ranch serving Christmas holiday dinners to three of the sexiest cowboys she's ever met!*

*Rafe, Brady and Dan thought they were getting male ex-cons to help out around their secluded ranch, but instead they get an attractive and very appealing female. In the snowbound wilds of Northern Ontario, female companionship is rare. It's a good thing the three men like to share...*

Christmas is coming once again to Moose Ranch and with the due date of JJ's baby approaching fast, JJ is distracting herself from anxiety attacks by keeping herself ultra-busy preparing for the arrival of her baby and planning Moose Ranch's first annual Christmas party!

In having a wee baby on the way, there's a lot of stress for Brady, Rafe and Dan. Especially due to JJ's decision on having a wilderness mid-wife deliver the baby at the ranch house - *with* all *of them present for the birth*! But their concerns don't stop the men from showing JJ how much they love her...out of bed and in!

With wicked snowstorms, a grounded bush plane, a cheerful holiday party and a sweet little baby, the owners of Moose Ranch know this will be one sparkling Christmas season they won't soon forget...

. . ⚜ . .

Her Forever Cowboys
Cowboys Online 6 ~ Snowy Creek Ranch
A Canadian Contemporary Ménage Romance m/f/m/m
Jan Springer

. . ⚜ . .

After spending years in prison, Milena Allen is unexpectedly paroled
and given a job at a secluded Canadian horse ranch where she's
instantly attracted to her three sexy cowboy bosses!
When Cowboys Online sends Mitch, Daegen and Paul a cute female
ex-con to help out around their fledgling wilderness ranch, they realize
life has been awfully lonesome without female companionship.
Despite being without women for so long, they vow Milena is off
limits, and they will treat her like one of the guys.
When violence threatens her cowboys, Milena's nursing skills are put
to the test, and she realizes she's falling head over cowboy boots for her

sexy bosses. Soon she discovers all three men are interested in her too! But they keep treating her like one of the guys!

She's always dreamed for someone to love her and for a place she can call home. Will Mitch, Daegen and Paul make her dreams come true? Or will a horrific mistake unravel everything?

• • ⌀ • •

YOU CAN GET A PEEK at more of Jan Springer's Erotic Romances at:

http://www.janspringer.com[1]

---

1.    http://www.janspringer.com/

# Here are ways we can connect

Jan Springer Website at http://www.janspringer.com[1]

Instagram – http://www.instagram.com/janspringerauthor

Facebook - https://www.facebook.com/janspringereroticromance

Twitter Jan Springer- https://twitter.com/janspringer @janspringer

Pinterest - http://www.pinterest.com/janspringer1/

Jan's Blog - http://janspringerauthor.wordpress.com/blog-2/

Happy Reading,

Jan Springer

---

1. http://www.janspringer.com/

# More Spunky Girl Publishing stories!

Jan Springer writing as Jasmine Black ~ Erotica without the Romance[1]
jasmine-black.com[2]
Jan Springer writing as Laura Kristina ~ Lesbian & Gay Attraction[3]
laurakristina.com

• • ∞ • •

Jan Springer ~ Reverse Harem & Erotic Romance[4]

---

1. http://www.jasmine-black.com

2. http://www.jasmine-black.com

3. http://www.laurakristina.com

4. http://www.janspringer.com

# Don't miss out!

Visit the website below and you can sign up to receive emails whenever Jan Springer publishes a new book. There's no charge and no obligation.

https://books2read.com/r/B-A-WGQ-ERWZB

Connecting independent readers to independent writers.

Did you love *Claiming Her Cowboys*? Then you should read *Her Forever Cowboys*[5] by Jan Springer!

After spending years in prison, Milena Allen is unexpectedly paroled and given a job at a secluded Canadian horse ranch where she's instantly attracted to her three sexy rancher bosses!

When Cowboys Online sends Mitch, Daegen and Paul, a lady ex-con to help out around their wilderness ranch, they realize life has been lonely without female companionship. Despite being deprived of women for so long, the men vow that Milena is off limits.

When violence threatens her cowboys, Milena's caring skills are put to the test, and she realizes she is falling head over straw hats for her sexy bosses. Soon she discovers all three men are interested in her too! But they keep treating her like one of the guys!

---

5. https://books2read.com/u/3nEnEo

6. https://books2read.com/u/3nEnEo

She's always wanted someone to love her and to have a place she can call her home. Can Mitch, Daegen and Paul make Milena's dreams come true? Or will a horrific mistake by Cowboys Online unravel everything?

Cowboys Online Series ~ Book One – Cowboys for Christmas (Moose Ranch), Book Two – Cowboys in Her Pocket (Moose Ranch), Book Three – Loving Her Cowboys (Moose Ranch), Book Four – Cowboys in Her Heart (Moose Ranch), Book Five – Always Her Cowboys (Moose Ranch), Book Six – Her Forever Cowboys (Snowy Creek Ranch).

Read more at www.janspringer.com.